D0427333

EAT BUGS
PROJECT
STARTUP

EAT BUGS
PROJECT
STARTUP

WITHDRAWN

BY HEATHER ALEXANDER
WITH LAURA D'ASARO AND ROSE WANG, THE FOUNDERS OF *CHIRPS*™
ILLUSTRATED BY VANESSA FLORES

**TO ELIZABETH BENNETT, WHO COOKED UP A BOOK FROM A
CRICKET CHIP AND BROUGHT US ALL TOGETHER—HA**

**TO THE NAI NAIS, BECAUSE BEHIND EVERY SUCCESSFUL ENTREPRENEUR
IS SOMEONE CRAZY ENOUGH TO BELIEVE IN THEM FIRST—LD + RW**

FOR GLADYS. THANKS FOR YOUR UNWAVERING ENCOURAGEMENT—VF

PENGUIN WORKSHOP
An Imprint of Penguin Random House LLC, New York

Text copyright © 2021 by Heather Alexander LLC, Laura D'Asaro, and Wei Wang.
Illustrations copyright © 2021 by Vanessa Flores. All rights reserved.
Published by Penguin Workshop, an imprint of Penguin Random House LLC, New York. PENGUIN
and PENGUIN WORKSHOP are trademarks of Penguin Books Ltd, and the W colophon is
a registered trademark of Penguin Random House LLC. Manufactured in China.

If you want to experiment with eating insects, please don't eat insects you catch in the wild.
You can purchase edible insects that are farmed and have gone through quality testing.
Also, if you are allergic to crustaceans or shellfish, you may also be sensitive to insects.

Visit us online at www.penguinrandomhouse.com.

Library of Congress Cataloging-in-Publication Data is available upon request.

ISBN 9780593096178

10 9 8 7 6 5 4 3 2 1

PROLOGUE
HALLIE

Have you ever heard of the butterfly effect?

A butterfly in Brazil flaps its wings, and that tiny motion creates small changes in the atmosphere. Those changes make other, bigger weather changes and so on until eventually a tornado barrels through some random town far away in Oklahoma. If you live there, your life literally gets turned upside down. And it's all because a small butterfly flapped its wings thousands of miles away.

One seemingly unimportant thing can make big changes.

That happened to me the first time I ate a bug. Everything changed. Not just for me—for Jaye, too.

Only we didn't know it then.

I've eaten a thousand bugs by now. I've had them fried and sautéed. I've baked them into cookies. I've mashed them into guacamole and sprinkled them on yogurt. I've had them with hot sauce, with melted cheese, and with chocolate. (When it comes to bugs, dark chocolate beats milk chocolate, in case you're wondering.)

My first bug was just a regular, plain bug. I hadn't planned to eat it. But sometimes you do a totally unexpected thing, and it sparks ideas and brings people together in wild ways.

As I said, total butterfly effect.

But with a cricket.

CHAPTER 1
HALLIE

"Ewww! That's the grossest thing *ever!*"

Even though I stood on the far side of the exhibit, it didn't take any great genius to know who was squealing. The chorus of giggles and gasps gave Erica Sanchez away. Erica is the girl in our grade who kids orbit around like backup singers, providing a soundtrack of constant approval.

"That chimp is picking bugs out of the other chimp's hair and *eating* them!" cried Erica.

All eyes turned to the three chimps sitting on the

tree limb. I chewed my lip as I watched them groom one another with their humanlike fingers. Their enclosure at the Brookdale Zoo was supposed to mimic a rain forest. I seriously doubted these chimps thought this was any kind of real rain forest.

I'm not sure how I feel about zoos. When I see the animals trapped inside the cages, I get supremely sad. But I do like watching them. Is that bad? I mean, they're just so amazing. The chimps have the sweetest-looking eyes.

The summer I was six, I visited the zoo all the time. Dad's a photographer, and he was working on a series that showed an animal in the zoo and then the same animal living the free life outdoors. Dad's photographs make statements. They're dramatic. Eye-opening. I like that. I'm all for making statements.

"Sanchez, don't move!" Spencer Montan screamed loud enough for the whole sixth grade to hear. He reached his finger into Erica's long, dark braid.

"I've got it." Spencer cupped his hands together. They twitched as if something inside was fighting to get free.

"What is it?" Erica's brown eyes widened with fear. "Was it *on* me?"

Spencer smirked mischievously, keeping his hands shut tight.

I edged closer.

"Ewww!" Samara Matthews shuddered dramatically.

"Gross," echoed Jaye Wu. She twisted a strand of her long black hair tightly around her finger.

Neither of them could've possibly seen what he'd captured, but that didn't matter. Jaye and Samara traveled in Erica's shadow, oohing and aahing as if on cue. From what I could tell, Jaye always seemed to be a beat behind Samara. Of course, I barely knew them. It was only the end of September, so most of us at Brookdale Middle School hadn't ventured far from our elementary-school groups.

Not that I've ever had a group. I'm not a group-friend kind of person.

It was always just me and Zara—we liked it like that. But Zara moved to Canada this summer. We tried to convince her parents not to go. We even painted a massive sign on a bedsheet that said "Let Zara Stay!" and hung it in front of their house. It was my idea to make a public statement.

It didn't work.

They went anyway and took Zara with them. So it's just me now.

I watched Spencer and Erica out of the corner of my eye. I was curious about what was jumping inside Spencer's hands.

"Do you want to see? One . . . two . . . three!" He raised his hands and opened them wide.

I didn't see anything. I blinked, sure I'd missed it.

"There's nothing there." Erica wrinkled her snub nose.

"Gotcha!" Spencer doubled over with laughter. "You totally fell for it, Sanchez."

"My man!" Raul Cortez slapped Spencer a high five.

Erica gave Spencer a playful shove. He grinned stupidly at her.

I turned back to the chimps. Spencer was an idiot.

"My students, over here." Mrs. Marcelli clapped her hands several times for attention. "We're heading to the Reptile Rotunda."

"My classes, follow me." Mrs. Stein didn't clap or raise her voice. The sixth-graders who had Mrs. Stein for science already knew not to mess with her. She was always complaining about the amount of material we had to cover. She banned questions that were off topic, because they ate into the time she'd allotted for the lesson.

That's a huge problem for me. I mean, why bother going to school if you can't ask questions? I could just sit home and read a book. Albert Einstein said it's important to be "passionately curious," and I totally agree. Guess who's my least favorite teacher?

Exactly.

"Where are we going?" I asked as I followed Mrs. Stein down several zoo pathways.

"The Bug House." Mrs. Stein stopped outside a terra-cotta building with a sign that exclaimed "Abuzz with Wonder!" She held up her hand like a traffic guard. "Wait for the others, Hallie."

I pulled my listbook and my cobalt blue pen from my backpack. School involves massive amounts of waiting and lining up, so I carry my listbook everywhere. It's a small black notebook with thick, creamy paper. My dad bought an enormous carton of them on sale years ago, and we've got dozens still piled in the corner of our dining room. I fill them with lists. Lists let you see everything swirling around in your brain.

I flipped back a few pages to the ones I'd made this week:

- **Mythical Creatures I Most Want to Meet**
(griffin is #1)
- **Most Excellent Condiments**
(sriracha pulls top honors)
- **Animals I'd Turn Into If I Could Shape-Shift**
(liger wins, but cheetah is a close second)

I started a new list:

Cool Things I Know about Insects

1. Their bodies have 3 parts: a head, thorax, and abdomen.

2. They have 6 legs. So spiders (8 legs!) and worms (no legs!) aren't insects.

3. They have 2 antennae.

← head
← thorax
← abdomen

"Why's it called a thorax?" I asked Mrs. Stein.

"I bet we can find someone inside who can answer you." Mrs. Stein pushed open the door.

I shut my listbook, tucked it into my backpack, and stepped into the darkness. My eyes took a minute to focus on the dozens of terraria set into the walls. Each housed different bugs—stick insects, ants, roaches, and beetles.

"Gather round, kids." A tall guy with wire-rimmed glasses and messy blond hair stood in the center of the large room. He wore a khaki shirt with the zoo's logo on the front. "I'm Dr. Bugatti, but everyone calls me Dr. Bug."

I laughed. So did a bunch of other kids.

"I'm an entomologist—that's a scientist who studies bugs," said Dr. Bug. "Everyone, be as quiet as you can and listen." A gradual chorus of buzzing and chirping rose up from the different corners of the room. Dr. Bug walked us past the different displays—a tarantula crawling on a rock, a praying mantis camouflaged by a leaf, and caterpillars that would soon transform into monarch butterflies.

My eyes kept going back to the enormous tarantula. It looked strangely cuddly, like a pet. I had this weird desire to touch its furry body. As I watched it take tiny steps, I completely tuned out Dr. Bug and the class as they examined colorful beetles. When I'm interested in something, I commit fully (sometimes too fully, my mom says).

"Okay, now my favorite part. Snack time!" announced Dr. Bug. "Who wants to eat insects?"

That got my attention. I whirled around to see Dr. Bug lift a small box off a shelf.

"Seriously? You want us to eat bugs?" Ava Baltimore shook her head so violently, her braids quivered.

"I do. They're delicious." Dr. Bug smiled broadly, but I could tell he wasn't joking. He held out the box, and we crowded closer. *Crickets* was written on the side in colorful bubble letters. A little window revealed small brown insects inside. "You may think this is strange, but it's not. Around the world, more people eat insects than speak English. They are an important and sustainable food source, especially as the world's population explodes and there's not enough clean water or land to feed so many humans. Think of crickets like land shrimp. Shrimp and lobster are really just giant sea bugs."

Erica groaned. "That doesn't help."

"What if they crawl around in your mouth?" asked Owen Locke.

"Won't happen, my friend. These crickets aren't alive. They've been fried and seasoned. As I said, they're quite delicious." Dr. Bug smacked his lips. "Any takers?"

Everyone grew very quiet. I stared at the box. I'd never considered eating a bug before, but I was curious what a cricket would taste like. Squishy? Crunchy?

My parents once took me to a French restaurant and ordered escargot (which is a fancy word for snails). I ate those in a butter-garlic sauce, and they weren't half-bad, so I figured there was no real difference. Besides, a bug is so tiny. Eating it didn't seem like a big deal.

I raised my hand and stepped forward. "I'll try one."

CHAPTER 2
JAYE

Who said that? I stood on my tiptoes, twisting toward the back of the room. I scanned all the faces. Who here would actually eat a cricket?

Spencer caught my eye and made a loud gagging noise. He didn't even trying to disguise it. Other kids snickered.

I knew Spencer would never consider eating a bug. He wasn't adventurous that way. He wouldn't even try the xiao long bao or the jellyfish noodles my grandma made for lunch.

I tried to remember the last time he'd been at my house. Sometime last spring? He'd spent the summer away with his family at a lake and then went to soccer camp with Raul, Owen, and a bunch of other boys. Since then, he stopped hanging out with me unless we were in a group. And ever since school started, he'd been acting so different. Saying mean things.

"Come on up here, young lady." Dr. Bug waved his arms, and we all cleared a path. Hallie Amberose confidently made her way toward the front.

"Figures," sneered Spencer. "Hallie's so weird."

"Tragically weird," added Raul.

Hallie's in my Business Education and Entrepreneurship class. She sits near the window. I've never spoken a word to her. Even so, I desperately wanted to reach out, grab her and warn her that this wasn't going to end well.

But I didn't. Instead, I shoved my hands deep into my hoodie pockets and held my breath. It was like watching a car roll backward down a hill. She'd have to save herself.

"What on earth is she wearing?" Erica whispered loudly.

"I know, right?" I answered before Samara could.

Hallie wore denim overalls with streaks of silver paint along the cuffs. A bright yellow fanny pack decorated with absurdly large rhinestones was slung low around her waist. Sharpie swirls covered her maroon Converse. Her face was barely visible behind a mess of chestnut curls.

I rolled my eyes. This girl was majorly weird. It was like she didn't care what anyone thought, which made absolutely no sense. I think about that all the time. Like every minute. Especially now that Spencer decided we should be part of Erica's group. I needed to know the right thing to say. The right emoji to choose. The right jeans to wear.

Spencer and I used to not care what we said or wore or did. But this year, Spencer's constantly declaring what's cool and what's not. So is Erica. I eyed Erica's powder-blue jeans and striped short-sleeve Henley top. I also wore pale jeans.

My top was solid navy, but the same style. I've made sure of that.

Even so, sometimes it feels like they don't remember I'm there. Or *not* there.

Last week, Erica, Samara, Spencer, and Raul met up for ice cream and never told me. Erica apologized. She said they just forgot to ask me. No big deal. Spencer never said anything. Did he forget me, too? How is that even possible when we've been best friends since kindergarten?

Hallie stopped in front of Dr. Bug. We crowded closer until I was right behind her. The ends of her hair smelled like raspberries.

Dr. Bug lifted the lid off the box. He plucked out a small, pale brown cricket and placed it into Hallie's outstretched hand.

The cricket was shriveled, but even in the dim light, its hard shell held a brilliant sheen.

Hallie inhaled sharply.

She's going to back out. I giggled. I do that when I'm nervous. Relief flooded through me. She'll pretend it was just a joke. It's what I'd do.

I took a giant step away from her.

Then Hallie popped the whole cricket into her mouth. I heard the *crunch* as she bit down.

"Ewww!"

"I can't even!"

"She ate it!"

The class erupted with gagging noises and groans. Mrs. Stein tried to restore order. She clapped her hands loudly.

Hallie swallowed, then grinned. "It's good. Really good. It tasted like a spicy peanut."

"Exactly right." Dr. Bug gave her a fist bump.

"Bug Girl ate a nasty cricket!" Spencer whooped and then pretended to vomit.

"Spencer, that's enough!" Mrs. Stein swooped in and pulled him off to the side.

Dr. Bug held out the box. "Anyone else?"

I wanted to step forward. Not to eat the crickets—I'd never do that. I just wanted to see them better. My parents are scientists, and I guess I get my curiosity from them.

I glanced over at Spencer, then over at Erica. For the rest of the year, Hallie would be "Bug Girl." Maybe for the rest of her life. I didn't need a label like that, too—it was enough that I was the only Chinese kid in the grade. I stayed where I was.

"No one else?" Dr. Bug shook his head in dismay, then presented the box to Hallie. "Lucky you. You get the rest to take home."

"Thanks!" She seemed genuinely excited. "It's a most excellent party favor."

Erica snickered. So did the rest of the kids.

I stepped far away from Bug Girl.

CHAPTER 3
HALLIE

As the school bus pulled away from the zoo, I examined the crickets through the box's clear cellophane window. They kind of looked like roasted nuts or mini pretzel sticks, definitely not worthy of all the intense drama. Even so, I was proud of myself for trying one.

I pulled out my phone.

u r not gonna believe what I just ate!!

a cricket!!!!!

I sent a picture of the bugs in the box.

I waited for Zara to text back. Then I realized that she was still in school and wouldn't have her phone on. I tucked mine back into my purple backpack so none of the teachers would see.

"Do you want one?" I extended the box to Lily Sullivan-Miller. Lily was perched so far off the edge of the bus seat we shared, she practically tumbled into the aisle each time the driver braked. Lily raised her hands as if protecting herself and cringed.

"Hey, it's not like the crickets are alive or anything." I turned around to Owen. I've known him since first grade, when he carried a stuffed tiger with only one ear to school every day and cried when Miss Carl made him put it in his backpack. "Want to try? The cricket really did taste like a spicy peanut. It's probably because of all the seasonings on it. Honestly, it's supergood—"

"Give it a rest, Hallie." Owen spoke through clenched teeth.

"I'll take one." A boy with curly brown hair who sat next to Owen reached out his hand. I didn't know his name.

"Sure thing!" I handed him a cricket. "Tell me what you think—"

I didn't get to finish.

"Incoming missile!" he hollered, then launched the cricket through the air. It landed on Raul's shoulder, and he tossed it toward another boy, who sent it flying down the aisle. It got tangled in Sophia DuPre's hair, and she let out an ear-piercing shriek. Mrs. Stein stood and went to find out what the fuss was about, and suddenly she was looming over me, lecturing me about how the crickets weren't toys and how if I didn't put them away, she'd have to take them from me.

I thought about telling her it was all that boy's fault, but instead I promised to keep the box in my backpack for the rest of the ride back to school. She nodded and let me keep the crickets.

That night, I placed the box in the middle of our kitchen table, right between a bowl of roasted broccoli and a platter of steaming penne.

Dad raised his bushy eyebrows. He has very expressive eyebrows. I can tell what he's thinking just by the way they move, and he was clearly intrigued. "Sharing your science project?"

"Nope." I shook my head. "Guess again."

"A little dinner music?" Mom spooned a heaping pile of mushy broccoli onto my plate. "*The Cricket's song, in warmth increasing ever.'* That's from Keats." Mom can quote a line of poetry that goes with whatever you say, no matter how random. I call it her weird superpower.

"What?" my older brother, Henry, asked. He reached for the penne.

"Crickets sing, Henry," Mom explained. "They rub their wings together to communicate, and it makes a song,"

"Technically, Marika, they don't sing," Dad corrected her. "Crickets chirp."

"Actually, Stan, only the male cricket chirps," Mom corrected him with a satisfied smirk.

"Actually—" Dad started.

"Whoa!" I interrupted. My parents could go on like this all night, if not stopped. They're always one-upping each other with random facts. It's the closest thing to a sport our unathletic family has. "It's not a cricket chorus. Guess again."

Henry handed Dad the penne and greedily pulled the box toward him. "You brought dinner for Randall."

Randall is our pet lizard. We also used to have a garter snake called Beasley, but Beasley kept escaping. Henry decided that Beasley needed to return to the wild, so we took Beasley to the nature preserve. We had a big send-off ceremony. Dad played "Leaving on a Jet Plane" on his ukulele. Mom quoted a poem about taking a journey. I blew bubbles, because I think bubbles are so happy and festive.

I grabbed my box back. "The crickets aren't dinner for Randall. They're dinner for *us*."

"Us? Are you saying something about my cooking?" Mom's supergood at art and computer graphics, but her cooking skills are majorly lacking.

"No, I'm saying we should all try a cricket tonight. I ate one today. On the field trip."

Dad's eyebrows lifted higher. "How was it?"

"Super tasty!"

"Why'd you do that?" Henry wrinkled his nose. "No one eats bugs."

"You're wrong. Lots of people do. All over the world," I shot back.

"Like where?"

"Like . . . everywhere." Okay, I didn't really know, but I wasn't about to tell him that. Henry's three years older and in high school, and he acts like he knows way more than I do. Which is probably true, but I didn't want to hear it.

"People in Asia eat bugs," said Mom. "Remember my college friend Anna? She tried a fried scorpion kebab when she was in Thailand. And Luisa at work is from Ghana. She's eaten caterpillars and something else. Mealworms, maybe?"

"People in South America and Mexico eat bugs, too," Dad jumped in. "I have two friends who've eaten termites seasoned with chili and lime."

"And here, too," added Mom. "Native Americans of the Onondaga Nation eat the cicadas that emerge every seventeen years. They cook them in butter and garlic."

"See?" I smiled at Henry and opened the box. "Everyone's doing it."

Henry poked at a cricket with the tines of his fork, inspecting it. He's constantly taking things apart—computers, toys, even the coffee maker. Random wires and springs litter the floor of our house. He stared at the cricket for a moment, then popped it into his mouth, chewed, and swallowed. "Tastes like sunflower seeds. Or a Dorito. Crunchy and kind of nutty."

Dad placed one in his palm and smelled it. He has a supersensitive nose. He insists 80 percent of the flavors we taste come from smell.

"It passes the smell test. Okay, down the hatch." He swallowed the cricket whole, then smacked his lips. *"Delicioso!"*

Mom squinted her hazel eyes, then ate one, too.

"Awesome, right?" I was so happy my whole family had tried them. Not that I was surprised. I mean, I had to get my curiosity from somewhere. "Let's toss a few into the pasta. Crickets have a lot of protein, and you're always saying I could use more of that."

I'm a vegetarian. It all started one night last year, after my family watched a documentary about how animals raised and killed for food are cruelly mistreated. That movie scarred me for life. Seriously. I bawled my eyes out throughout the whole thing. From that moment on, I made a rule: I won't eat anything cute and cuddly or anything that feels pain. Broccoli doesn't feel pain. Neither do chocolate chip cookies. And cheese doesn't cuddle.

"Wait!" I caught my breath. "What about insects? Do

they feel pain? Can I be vegetarian and still eat them?"

Dad scratched his thick beard, and Mom shrugged. I grabbed the tablet from the pile of unopened mail on our kitchen counter and began to research.

"Whew!" I had scrolled through several pages. "It says here that most insects don't feel pain. They don't suffer. So I can be an entotarian—a person who eats vegetables *and* bugs. Besides, insects aren't cute or cuddly. You can't hug bugs."

"What does hugging have to do with whether it's morally correct to eat them?" Henry challenged, leaning forward. He turns everything into a debate.

"Hugging has a lot to do with it. We all step on and squish bugs. I kill mosquitoes. That doesn't bother me, so why should eating them?"

"Then why isn't everyone eating them?" Henry narrowed his gaze at me. We share the same gray-green eyes, but his nose and chin are sharper. So is his tongue, my dad likes to joke.

"I don't know." I searched for more facts. "Wait . . . actually, every person eats one to two pounds of bugs every year without knowing it. They're little hitchhikers. They climb onto vegetables and fruits. They get into salads and juices. It says here they're even in some chocolate."

That night I kept on researching bugs instead of helping Mom with our latest craft project. We do a new one every month. Right now, we're smashing floral china plates we found at a yard sale and tiling a funky mosaic pattern on our old wooden coffee table. But Mom understood. She completely supports "deep dives." That's when you find out everything you can on one subject.

And I couldn't stop thinking about bugs. Not only crickets, but *all* bugs.

Who knew these little guys were so fascinating?

Cool Things about Bugs

There are sooooo many bugs in the world! Over 1 million different species!!!

Bugs have been on Earth for over 400 million years—*way* before the dinosaurs.

Grasshoppers have ears on their stomachs!

Ants are wicked strong. They can lift 5,000 times their own weight. That's like me carrying a blue whale.

CHAPTER 4
JAYE

I opened my notebook and leaned closer to Erica's and Samara's desks. Mr. Thompson scribbled furiously on the whiteboard, his green marker squeaking. He didn't seem to care that everyone was talking while he had his back to us.

"Don't you think so?" Samara asked me. She and Erica were debating some new music video.

I chewed a hangnail on my thumb and nodded enthusiastically. I'm the queen of the silent nod—I nod when I have no idea what to say. Which is often.

Hurry up and teach, I silently urged Mr. Thompson. I hadn't seen the music video, and I didn't want to risk saying something stupid. Erica and Samara thought I was way more plugged-in than I really was.

All sites where I'd possibly watch anything cool are blocked in my house. My parents insist the "nonsense" will destroy my brain and take away from my studies. The thing is, I'd spend *more* time doing my homework if I didn't have to scheme ways to memorize lyrics so I could randomly quote them to pretend I knew the songs everyone knows.

When I was five, I moved to upstate New York from our small town in China. I didn't know anything about what kids in America liked. Zero. Not even Disney or LEGO. Luckily, Spencer lived across the street. I'd spend hours at his house watching TV, playing on his computer, and listening to music.

Or I used to do that. I miss him, but that makes no sense, since he's sitting right behind me.

Mr. Thompson pounded his desk with his hands. "Drumroll, everyone!"

The thunder of twenty pairs of hands vibrated the metal desks against the linoleum floor. Then Mr. Thompson pushed the sleeves of his faded denim shirt up to his elbows and pointed to the board.

"Our big project," he announced dramatically.

He'd written *PITCH! The Ultimate Kid-preneurship Pitch Competition.*

I grinned. I'd wanted to take Culinary Explorations for my elective, because you got to make and eat mac and cheese. But when my parents heard that Mr. Thompson had run his own successful advertising company and then sold it, they made me sign up for Business Education and Entrepreneurship, also called BEE. School had started only a month ago, but already Mr. Thompson's class was my favorite. He treats us like we're working at a cool company and not stuck in a classroom.

"Okay, class. We're embarking on a project to teach you the skills to start and grow a business." Mr. Thompson paced when he spoke. He's really tall, so he can take only a few steps one way before he's across the classroom and has to turn back. "Remind me again. What's a business?"

"A business is when someone makes, buys, and sells goods or services," Raul recited.

"Exactly. And an entrepreneur is someone who's brave enough to dream up something new—something no one else has dared to try—and build it into a business. That will be *you*. You will be an entrepreneur with your own startup company." Mr. Thompson was a little out of breath from all his pacing and excitement. "You will do everything you'd do if you had a real business. Make a product, test it, advertise it, and sell it. One month from now, you will give a pitch to a panel of judges here at Brookdale Middle School. A pitch is a presentation to convince someone that your business will be a success. The best pitch wins."

"Is there a prize?" Lily called out. Mr. Thompson's the only teacher who doesn't make us raise our hands. He believes it stops the natural flow of ideas.

"You know it." Mr. Thompson grinned. "The winner gets two hundred dollars *and* will go on to compete in the county competition against teams from other schools. The state competition and the national competition follow. But *first* you must win our competition."

"That will be me," Raul announced.

Spencer snorted. "Not a chance. I don't know if you know, but my uncle Gabe created the app Candy Connxt, and—"

The entire class groaned.

"We *all* know," Raul said. "You've told us like a bajillion times."

"What can I say? Entrepreneurship runs in my family. Fame, too," Spencer boasted. "I'm buying an electric scooter with the prize money."

Everyone started talking about the cool things they'd buy if they won.

I knew exactly what I'd get. An outfit from Sparks, the boutique on Olcott Street. My parents drive all the way out to Highway 34 to buy our clothes at BargainWays. They insist BargainWays is just as good, but they're clueless when it comes to fashion. They're always saving and saving. They say that's the Chinese way. That makes no sense. They moved to America, so shouldn't we live—and spend—like Americans?

"You've got it wrong, folks!" Mr. Thompson called out.

"The prize money isn't yours personally. You don't get to buy new scooters with it."

After we finished moaning, he explained that PITCH! worked like a ladder. If you win the school competition, the rule is you have to invest the money in your company to make it better and grow it. Then you climb up a rung and compete in the next competition. And if you win that money, you use it again and move up and up until you're competing on the national level.

I liked the idea of a national competition.

I can totally win, I decided. *I'm good at school. How hard can it be to pitch a business?*

I imagined my winning photo up on every news site. I'd be looking super professional in a crisp business suit. My parents would brag to all our relatives—their daughter had done something important! They were always saying how they wish someday they could work for themselves. I could do that *now*. Make them proud.

"There's no textbook for this. We'll learn by doing." Mr. Thompson's voice broke through my thoughts. "You're all going to make mistakes, and then learn from those mistakes."

I didn't want to make any mistakes. I wanted to win. If I won, Erica and Spencer would be impressed. My parents, too.

I'd be unforgettable.

"First up, you'll work in pairs." Chair legs scratched as we twisted and turned. I quickly looked to Erica, but she'd already paired with Samara. "Sorry," she mouthed with an apologetic shrug.

I immediately shifted my gaze to Spencer. In elementary school, we'd worked together on every group project. I don't make a big deal when he goofs off, and he lets me be bossy. We're great partners. But Raul, Dion, and Owen were huddled around Spencer, and they quickly paired off. Spencer never once looked my way. Around the classroom, teams rapidly formed.

"Sit back down, folks. I will be picking your partners,"

Mr. Thompson boomed. I quietly exhaled. Mr. Thompson liked me. He'd give me someone good.

He began to read off the pairs. Finally, he called my name. "Jaye Wu . . . you will start a business with Hallie Amberose."

Spencer snickered loudly behind me. "Bug Girl," he whispered in my ear. "You got Bug Girl."

Seriously? I didn't want to be the weird girl's partner.

Mr. Thompson instructed us to start brainstorming, and before I knew it, Hallie was hurrying over with a wide smile on her face.

"Hey there, pitch partner! Are you ready to do this? It's like *Shark Tank*, but at school, right? I have so many great ideas! Do you?" She scooted an empty desk over so it touched mine. I shrank back and glanced to the side. Erica and Lily were whispering together. I heard Spencer laugh behind me.

"I'm Hallie, but I guess you know that, since Mr. T just called our names." She stuck out her hand. I stared at it, unsure. Did she want us to shake? What kid did this? I didn't put my hand out.

"Jaye." I mumbled my introduction.

"I know!" Hallie pulled her hand back, not caring that I hadn't touched it. "So how do you like to brainstorm?"

I blinked. "Excuse me?"

"Are you a list girl like me? Or do you freestyle your

thoughts as they come to you? My brother does that. Or are you a visual thinker? My mom sketches her ideas, but that's because she thinks with the right side of her brain, because she's an artist." Hallie opened a small black notebook and searched for a blank page.

I hadn't ever thought about it before. "I guess I like to write lists."

"Excellent! We'll be the best partners!" She smiled enthusiastically, and before I could stop myself, I smiled back.

Then I noticed Erica look our way. I rearranged my expression and gave a sheepish wave. Erica waved back, then rolled her eyes. I swallowed hard and turned back to Hallie. She was writing in her notebook in big loopy letters.

Brainstorm with Jaye—Our FABULOUS ideas!

"I want to win," I burst out, surprising myself with the force of my words.

"Me too." Hallie raised her hand for a high five, and

I tentatively touched it. "And we will, because I have the world's best idea! Are you ready? It will blow you away!"

I nodded. I liked how Hallie spoke in exclamation points.

She leaned in even closer. "We create a product that gets more people to eat bugs."

"What?" I blinked. "Why would we want to do that?"

"Because bugs are amazing. Truly! And they're so healthy and—"

"I'm not doing that."

"But there are so many ways to eat them and—"

"No go. Not happening." I could only imagine what Spencer and Erica would say.

"But . . ." Hallie chewed her bottom lip. The bell rang at that moment.

"No bugs," I said forcefully, but when Hallie widened her eyes, I softened my voice. "We'll make a list of ideas, like you said."

We filed out of the classroom and into the hall. I slowed

my pace, watching as Hallie was pulled forward into the crowd.

Why was that girl so bug obsessed? If I wanted to win, I needed to do this myself. Tonight I'd make an awesome list of business ideas. And none would be creepy-crawly!

CHAPTER 5
HALLIE

On Tuesday, I watched Jaye twirl a strand of her hair around her finger. She was listening to Mr. T, but her gaze darted rapidly about the classroom, cataloging everyone's motions. She reminded me of an insect using its long thin antennae. Insects do everything with their antennae—feel, smell, taste, and hear. That's how they piece together what's happening.

Jaye's a carpenter ant, I decided. Not a queen ant, but an intense worker ant.

Last night at dinner, I made us all go around and choose what kind of insect we were most like. Mom was a butterfly. Dad was a dragonfly. Henry was a praying mantis. Henry said I'm a bumblebee, but I think I'm a ladybug. Both are colorful, but I'd never sting anyone. I'm totally against violence.

Oh yeah . . . I'm still majorly obsessing over bugs.

I jiggled my leg impatiently, eager to share my business ideas with Jaye. I'd made a long list. Bug eating was still my favorite by far, but I'd come up with others.

They were about bugs, too.

Mr. T had rearranged our desks so partners sat next to each other. He pointed to Samara and Jazmina. "You're starting a business. What kind?"

"We're going to bake brownies and sell them," Samara offered.

"Brownies, good. But why?"

"Why?" Samara's gaze shifted uneasily to her partner, Jazmina. "We like brownies."

"I like brownies, too. But what's so great about *your* brownies?" Mr. T perched on the edge of his desk. "When you're brainstorming, don't start with the product, like brownies. Start with a problem that needs to be solved. A lemonade stand on a hot day solves the problem of thirsty people who want a cool drink. It wouldn't make much sense to have a lemonade stand in a snowstorm. Or to sell hot chocolate during a heat wave. What problems can brownies solve?"

"Hunger?" Sophia answered.

"You want something sweet?" suggested Owen.

"Good, but I can satisfy my sweet tooth by buying an ice-cream cone or choosing any number of brownies sold in the store. What's so special about *your* brownies?" he prodded. "Let's get more creative, folks."

"Their brownies can be super healthy," I suggested. "Like with the protein powder my mom puts in pasta sauce and pancakes."

Mr. T rubbed his palms together. "Now we're cooking. Someone expand on Hallie's idea."

"Maybe brownies can have carrots baked into them to get kids to eat more veggies? Lots of little kids don't like vegetables, but they like brownies," Bhavik Patel said.

"That's the problem-solution thinking I'm after. What other problems can the brownies solve?"

"How about brownies for dogs?" asked Lily. "I just got a puppy. She's the cutest brown labradoodle ever."

"Don't you know anything, Lily? Chocolate kills dogs. You'll go to jail for killing everyone's pets," Raul declared.

Lily widened her eyes. "Really?"

"But you could bake brownies with ingredients that are safe for dogs." Jaye flashed Lily an encouraging smile. I liked how she did that.

"Dogs don't need brownies," Bhavik argued.

"That's not true. My dog hates to take his medicine. It would be cool if I could tuck a pill inside the brownie and trick him into eating it. That solves a problem," Erica said.

"It sure does." Mr. T bounced to his feet. "In business, problems are also called pain points. The best products or services address pain points. You can create something that has never existed, or you can take something that's been around for a long time—like a hamburger—and change it or add to it to make it better."

"Like the new turkey burger special with extra jalapeños at Burger Barn!" called out Owen.

"So good." Mr. T patted his belly. "Did you know that when the first cell phones came out, the only thing you could do was make a call? That's it. Nothing else. Then someone thought, 'While I wait for my call, wouldn't it be cool if I could play a game?' and that person created games to play on our phones. Then someone else said, 'I want to tell my friend where to meet, but I don't want to have a long conversation,' and the idea of texting was born. Then someone else said, 'I want to show my friend I'm happy without writing a whole long thing,' and the smiley-face emoji came into being. The possibilities are endless. Let's spend a few minutes with our pitch partners identifying pain points and sharing ideas."

Jaye turned to me, carefully unfolding a piece of lined paper. "We should create something with technology. That's what Spencer's uncle Gabe did with Candy Connxt." She touched her finger to her tiny writing. "My first idea is a social media app to connect all the kids at Brookdale."

"Connect how?"

"Like a special app where you can chat and play games."

"Doesn't that already exist?"

"Ours will be special. You can only use it if you go to school here."

"What problem does it solve?"

Jaye folded her arms across her chest. "You don't have to be like that."

"Like what? It's what Mr. T said we

needed to do." I wasn't trying to crush her idea, but I didn't get what made it special.

Her glance darted toward Erica, who had her head down brainstorming with Lily, then returned to me. "The problem is that we don't all know each other, and sometimes it's easier to talk to someone digitally instead of going up to them in the hall."

"I get that. But . . ." I paused, reminding myself not to be harsh. I barely knew Jaye, after all. "But I can't see myself wanting to connect with"—my gaze skipped to Raul, then Spencer—"lots of kids here."

"Why not?" Jaye challenged. "What if you had something in common you didn't know about? An app could include everyone. A big group conversation. No one would be left out. It would demolish cliques. See? That's the problem *and* the solution."

"Okay." She was definitely passionate. I respected that, even if I didn't like the idea so much. I found a fresh page in my listbook. "Let's put it on our Maybe List."

"It's way better than a Maybe." Jaye sniffed.

She read off the rest of her ideas. A virtual closet. A site where you ranked the cafeteria food. A homework checklist. We agreed the school social network was the best of them.

"Bugs as food," I said when it was my turn.

"Are you kidding me? Not again." Jaye shook her head.

"Come on, it solves so many pain points. Lots of people, especially vegetarians, don't eat enough protein. That's just one problem eating bugs solves. Then there's the environment and—"

"Seriously, Hallie, I'm telling you, like *really* telling you, it's weird and gross. That Facebook guy built his own social network, and now he's a mega-billionaire. We *need* an app to win."

"Just because it's not techy doesn't mean it's a bad idea," I said.

I was surprised at how stubborn Jaye was being. I'd

figured once she heard my bug facts and grasped the pure awesomeness, she'd go along. But I couldn't get her to listen to me.

We sat in silence. I didn't like her idea. She didn't like mine.

The other kids were brainstorming loudly around us.

" . . . we'll make beaded bracelets and have people pick out the color of the beads . . ."

" . . . we can hire local restaurants to deliver lunch to school . . ."

" . . . we can make squirrel leashes and train squirrels to be pets . . ."

Jaye caught my eye, and we started to giggle. Once we started, it was hard to stop. Squirrel leashes? Even our worst ideas were way better than that!

"Take a look." I pushed my listbook toward her.

She flipped the pages curiously, eyeing all my doodles. "Is this book all lists?"

"It's a thing I do." I turned to the list I'd written last night.

♡   Eat Bugs, Not Burgers! ♡♡

Bugs need very little water/Cows need a lot.

- It takes 2,000 gallons of water to make 1 pound of beef (that's enough to fill a small swimming pool!).

- It takes 1 gallon of water to make 1 pound of crickets. DO THE MATH!

There are enough bugs to feed everyone on Earth/There aren't enough cows to feed everyone.

- Bugs cure hunger!

Cow farts make our planet warmer/Bugs don't fart (at least, I don't think so).

- Eating bugs saves Earth!

Cows are cute/Bugs are not.

Jaye's brown eyes grew darker. I could actually see her thinking.

"It's good, right?" My heart beat faster as I recited even more bug facts. "We can make a difference. Feed the world and—"

"Hallie, stop." Jaye sounded exasperated. "That's all true, but no one wants to eat bugs. You're the only one who even tried one."

"That doesn't mean . . . ," I trailed off.

Just like that, Jaye's attention had shifted to Spencer and Bhavik cracking a joke. As if what I was saying didn't matter.

"Narrow down on your best idea," Mr. T called out.

"A social network for the school," Jaye said firmly to me. "We're doing that."

I didn't answer. What was the point?

I'll work on the bugs at home, I decided. *It's better this way. It's too amazing an idea to be a school project.*

Anyone who was paying attention could see that.

CHAPTER 6
JAYE

I was surprised to see Owen and Raul scramble off the bus with Spencer a couple of days later. Spencer had joined the cross-country team, so he now took the late bus home. I'd been the only one at our stop for weeks.

"No practice?" I asked as we stood in Spencer's driveway.

"Coach had to go to a teachers' meeting." Raul lifted the lid of his baseball cap and pushed back the swoop of dark hair that covered his eye. He gazed at me suspiciously. I always got the sense Raul doesn't like me, but I didn't know why. "You live near here?"

Raul and Owen didn't go to elementary school with us, so they didn't know I lived across the street. I pointed to my blue-shingled house. My house and Spencer's both look exactly like the houses little kids draw. Rectangle bottom, triangle roof, window on either side of the front door. Spencer's lawn has lots of flowers, but we have only a few tomato plants. My dad thinks flowers are a waste. Vegetables look pretty, *and* they can be eaten.

"We're going inside to watch *Night of the Crimson Creature*, right, Spencer?" Raul rubbed his hands together in anticipation. "I heard there's a diabolical monster that comes out of the bathtub drain that's so freaky!"

"Beware! I vill make your blood boil and your heart freeze." Owen let out a maniacal laugh, as if he were a mad scientist. He's always doing funny accents. He can speak in a great robot voice, too.

"Word is the movie's total gore." Spencer looked down.

"You know, we can skip it if you guys can't handle it."

"Them?" I snorted. "Spence, you can't watch that." He hated anything scary. The first time he watched a *Harry Potter* movie, he'd had nightmares about Voldemort and slept with the hall light on for weeks.

Spencer glared at me. "You don't know what you're talking about, Jaye. "

I blinked in surprise. Why was he so angry?

"Let's go watch it, dudes." Spencer stalked up his front path. Raul and Owen hurried to catch up.

Should I follow? I'd normally just go in, but suddenly I wasn't so sure. I swallowed the lump forming in the back of my throat.

At that moment, Milo turned his red Toyota into the driveway. He climbed out of the car, nearly bumping his head. I hadn't seen Spencer's oldest brother for so long. He looked really grown-up now.

He waved. "Hey, JeeJee!"

I smiled at the nickname he'd given me long ago.

My Chinese name is Jie. When I moved here, my kindergarten teacher, Ms. Milton, called me "Jaye," even though it's pronounced "Jyeh." I barely spoke any English and didn't know the words to correct her, so the name stuck. A couple of months later, Milo, who was in fifth grade at the time, found out. He marched up to Ms. Milton at recess and told her she'd botched my name. She was embarrassed, but I told her I wanted to keep being Jaye.

Milo thought that was ridiculous. "It's not your name. It's not who you are," he insisted.

But he was wrong. I wanted to be Jaye. I even changed the spelling so it was easier for everyone to say. Being Jaye made me feel like I fit in.

"Aren't you coming in?" Milo asked me.

"Nah, I gotta go." I forced myself to walk as naturally as I could up my front path.

What was *that*? How could Spencer not invite me in?

Why was he acting so horrible this year? Everything was changing, and not in a good way.

I wished we were back in elementary school. Back then, our friendship had been as easy as breathing. Now I had to think about it. Worry about it.

I pushed open my front door, and the air was hot and heavy. The autumn breeze hadn't been allowed to worm its way inside, a sure signal that Nai Nai wasn't home to open windows. I kicked off my white sneakers, lining them perfectly parallel along the wall with all our other shoes. I slid on my gray felt slippers and padded toward the kitchen.

"Jie? Is that you?" My mother's soft voice startled me. It was strange for her to be home in the afternoon.

I found her making a sandwich. Her motions were precise and measured. Her brow furrowed slightly, as if the placement of every slice of cheese mattered.

"Mama, why aren't you at the lab?" I asked in Mandarin as I dropped my backpack onto a chair.

"I needed to bring Eddie his extra racket. He broke a string. Nai Nai is at the tennis courts with him." She placed the sandwich into a plastic container. Her long narrow fingers sealed the lid tightly. "I'm going back to work. Baba and I will be there late."

My parents worked together at a biochemistry lab. They were trying to discover how to make people sleep better. It had something to do with circadian rhythms, which are like clocks that we have inside ourselves. They sometimes stayed long into the night, because they needed to run tests around the clock.

Spencer's family always ate dinner together and spent entire Sundays chilling out and watching sports on their enormous sectional sofa. Not us. When my parents were home, they didn't ever relax. Lab reports. House repairs. Emails to friends and family in China. Taking us to Chinese school.

But Spencer's mom and dad were born here, so it's

different. It wasn't easy for Mama and Baba. They'd studied all the time when they were young to get into Yunnan University. That's where they met. They convinced Dr. Yang Han, an important scientist, to sponsor them to come to America. It took a long time to happen. When they finally managed to save up enough money and their work visas came through, I'd just been born. They couldn't travel to a new country (where they barely spoke the language) for big important jobs with a newborn baby to care for.

So they went without me.

For my first five years, I stayed with Nai Nai and Ye Ye, my grandparents, in China. Our apartment was cozy. I remember holding Ye Ye's calloused hand tightly as we fed the ducks in the evenings in the park across the street. Lots of other kids in our building lived with their grandparents, and I didn't miss my parents or even think about them. They called every Sunday, but all I remember about that is Baba's voice telling me stories of Mei Ming, a peacock that traveled to different faraway places. I learned later that he'd made up the stories to keep me on the phone, because I wouldn't answer any questions they asked. Truthfully, I was scared of their calls. At the time, I never really understood who they were.

Then Ye Ye had a heart attack and died. Nai Nai and I cried for a really long time. My dad had her bring me to America, and she planned to go right back to live with my auntie Biyu, but when we got here, Mama was pregnant with Eddie. She needed Nai Nai's help, so Nai Nai stayed. Besides, Nai Nai was lonely without my grandfather.

Nai Nai still talks about going back to China. I hate when she does that. I won't let her leave. Ever. In fourth grade, we had to write a simile about a member of our family, and I said Nai Nai was like a comfy, fluffy seat cushion cradling me from the hard, wooden furniture. When my teacher asked what the furniture represented, I shrugged and said it was just something I'd made up. But I did know.

My parents. They still felt like strangers.

"Did you have a test in science?" Mama handed me an orange.

"Yes. There was only one question I wasn't sure about." I recited the question on photosynthesis, and she agreed that the answer I'd chosen was correct.

Then we fell into silence. We never talk in paragraphs. A sentence here and there is the best we can do. I dug my fingernail deep into the orange rind and began to peel. Mama tucked a stray piece of hair into her low ponytail. She wears her hair the same way every day—along with the same style khakis and a dark-colored blouse. I always know what to expect from her, yet I never know what to say.

When I asked Nai Nai about it, she said that Mama's just not a "people person." I guess that's true. She's the quietest one in our family. But I also think it might have to do with all the time we spent apart. Every time I walk into the room, she frowns ever so slightly, as if she's confused by my being here. Nai Nai doesn't see it, but I do.

"Nai Nai will be back after Eddie's tennis lesson." Without saying anything more, she tucked the sandwich container into her quilted bag, changed into her outside shoes, and locked the front door behind her.

And I was alone in the familiar quiet.

I lined up the orange segments on the table. I ate one after each homework problem. I finished two math worksheets and circled an answer to go over with Baba. When I'm stumped, Baba sits with me and draws the equations. He's very patient, showing me every step. Finally, I pulled out the BEE assignment.

To complete it the way Mr. Thompson wanted involved

texting or talking to Hallie.

I rested my chin in my hand, thinking about her. She'd worn a red T-shirt today with a paper doily heart sewn with pink embroidery thread onto its center. It looked like a preschooler's Valentine's Day project. Had she made that herself? Why? And her Converse weren't decorated with the usual Sharpie hearts and stars. She'd drawn intricate paisleys and winding strawberry vines that, when I saw them up close, were actually kind of awesome.

But still . . .

She was so overly enthusiastic.

I couldn't puzzle her out. I reached into my backpack for a square of thin blue origami paper. I folded it in half and then in half again as I thought about Hallie. I ran my thumbnail over the creases and added an accordion fold. My fingers methodically lifted, then flattened the corners. In minutes, a tiny paper bird rested in the palm of my hand. I smiled, then tucked it into the side pocket of my backpack, where it joined four other origami birds, a frog, a fox, and a mangled mouse.

I'd made them all today.

This summer, I'd found a book in the library about this Japanese girl who made one thousand paper cranes, and I decided to try. I folded more than two hundred cranes before I moved onto other animals. Spencer wasn't around, so I had a lot of time by myself to make them. And, I don't know why, but folding squares of paper makes that fluttery feeling I sometimes get in my stomach not feel so bad.

Mama and Baba don't have any idea how many I've made. They haven't seen the big box filled with paper animals in the back of my closet.

Owen's loud laugh made me look out the kitchen window. The three boys kicked a soccer ball in the street. *So much for the movie!*

I watched for the longest time, until I couldn't take it anymore. Then I strolled outside, pretending I didn't see them. I focused on opening the mailbox and pulling out the mail.

"Coming your way, Jaye!" Spencer tapped the ball to me.

I trapped it and passed it to Raul. He passed it to Owen. Spencer showed off his bicycle kick, and just like that, we were back to normal. I didn't bring up the movie, because I didn't want him to get mad again.

"Guess what Hallie wants to do for our business," I said instead. "Bugs! She wants everyone to eat bugs!"

Spencer laughed and slapped his leg, like I knew he would. "What's her deal?"

I shrugged. "We're not going to do it. I have a way better idea."

"It's not the worst thing—" Owen started.

"Yeah it is," Spencer insisted. "What're you doing?"

"An online video homework service. Every day after school, we'll reteach the lessons using special effects. You know, wild graphics. Kids who were absent or didn't understand it the first time would totally buy it. Don't you think?" Owen asked.

"I do." I was really impressed. I turned to Raul. "What about you?"

"Peter and I are designing a summer sled," Raul said. "Lots of places don't have snowy winters, so kids miss out on all the sledding fun. We're making a sled that will kind of look like a big skateboard but instead of wheels, you attach special blocks of ice."

"And then what?" Spencer asked.

"You can sled down a grassy hill in the middle of summer! The sled will come with containers to freeze and mold the ice blocks." He was so busy explaining, he overkicked the ball, and it rolled past Owen and down our street. As Owen chased after it, Raul answered his phone. From his side of the conversation, I could tell it was his mom. He grimaced and walked off to talk to her.

"Want to hear my idea? A social network app just for our school," I told Spencer. "If you're in the school directory, you're automatically in it. And it will be totally safe, because no weird adults or kids from other schools can get in. Kids can share pics and . . . they can write only positive comments."

I just thought of that. My brain was whirring now.

"There'll be announcement boards for when someone is going to Burger Barn or for ice cream or to the park, and you can join, if you want." I was on a roll. "And there'll be games we all play together. Oh, and we'll each have our own avatar."

"You don't know how to code. How are you going to make an app?" Spencer folded his arms.

I hadn't thought about that part yet. "Does Milo code? Can he help me?"

Spencer snorted. "Good luck with that."

"Too bad your uncle Gabe isn't visiting," I said. "He'd know how for sure."

"What's your and Bhavik's business?" Owen asked Spencer after he'd run back with the ball and Raul had tucked his phone into his pocket.

"As if I'd tell."

"Come on," I said. "I bet it's an app, too. Right?"

"Top secret. All I can say is . . . it's on another level." Spencer flashed his familiar lopsided grin. "You'll have to wait. It'll blow your minds. *Boom!* I'm taking first place."

"Not happening," I taunted. I was sure *my* idea would come out on top. What could go wrong?

CHAPTER 7
HALLIE

Jaye texted.

I texted back.

I leaned into my big tie-dyed pillow and stared up at the paper monarch butterflies I'd pasted on my bedroom ceiling last year. Jaye kept on texting. Long paragraphs about how she'd brainstormed some more great components. She went on and on. She was really excited.

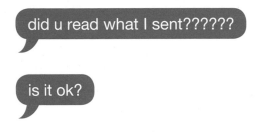

did u read what I sent??????

is it ok?

great

I wasn't sure why I wrote that. I didn't think it was great. Jaye had done our homework without even asking me, even though Mr. T said we were supposed to do it together.

She'd written that going to middle school is scary and confusing for some kids. She told a story about seeing these kids not knowing where to sit in the lunchroom or not being invited to ice cream on the weekend and feeling badly for them. She said the message boards and games on our app would include *all* kids in our school and bring us together for different kinds of activities.

Mr. T had said that in our pitch, we should tell a personal story to get people excited about our idea. It helps make the pain point feel real and urgent. Was Jaye's story personal?

Jaye was definitely part of the popular group and, in a strange way, not part of it—at the same time. I didn't really understand it.

Then I wondered if it was about me. With Zara gone, I sat by myself at lunch and read a book. But I didn't need an app to find a new friend. I'd already sized up everyone at Brookdale Middle School. No one could replace Zara. Not even close.

Besides, it was none of Jaye's business that I had no one to sit with.

I'll do the 1st part & u do the 2nd??

Each team had to present their idea in front of the class tomorrow. Mr. T would let us know if it was good—or if we had to come up with something new.

I stared up at my paper butterflies. My mom had taped them so their wings fluttered when a breeze floated through my open window. When I couldn't sleep, I'd play a game, pretending they were on an epic migration and needed to battle all these wild forces, like hurricanes and witches and Greek gods.

Suddenly I had an idea.

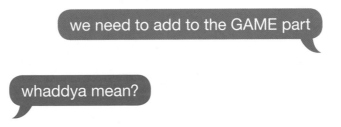

With one idea building upon the other, we transformed our business from a social media app into a scavenger hunt/relay race that only worked if everyone in school did their part. We still needed to figure out all the levels and a lot of other stuff, but when Jaye's grandmother cut us off to get ready for bed, I was smiling.

It felt more like *our* idea now.

The next day, Jaye walked into BEE with Spencer. They were deep in conversation, and she was talking rapidly. Erica and Samara appeared, and Spencer quickly took off with Bhavik. Jaye nodded at something Erica said. Not once did she look over at me.

Bug Eaters Around the World

Where	What	Supposedly Tastes Like
Mexico	grasshopper tacos (called chapulines)	salt & vinegar potato chips
Australia	bbq witchetty grubs (it's really moth larvae)	scrambled eggs
Nigeria	fried termites	bacon
Amazon Rainforest	raw rainforest ants	sour lemon candies

I turned back to the list in my listbook. Even though I'd agreed to the social media game with Jaye, I hadn't given up on my bugs.

"Okay, listen up!" Mr. T started class, and Jaye slid into her seat beside me. "Each team will stand at the front and explain their business. Short and sweet. This is not a pitch. But I want to see that you've put some real thought in. Erica and Lily, let's hear what you've got."

Erica and Lily planned to create a binder-decorating kit to allow kids to express themselves in school. Dion and Sophia came up with a sports jersey swap site. Samara and Jazmina had pivoted to brownies baked with vegetables. Ava and Zach wanted to design personalized bike helmets.

"Ours is so much better," Jaye whispered to me.

"It is." We shared conspiratorial grins.

"Okay . . . okay . . . okay . . . so imagine this," Spencer began slowly when it was his and Bhavik's turn. "You go to Brookdale Middle School. You know some kids in your class but not others. You're a little shy or nervous or whatever. How will you make friends? *Boom!* Just by going to school here, you're part of our new, super-awesome school-wide social network game. First, you design your own awesome avatar. Then you're each given a secret item that will be needed later . . ."

My head snapped to look at Jaye. Her lips were pressed together as if she were trying hard not to explode with what we were both thinking.

Spencer and Bhavik were presenting our idea!

Jaye must have told him about the game and the rules we'd created. He'd added a few things of his own, but it was so clearly our idea. Come on! Who does that? What a thief!

I nudged Jaye with my elbow. Her gaze was frozen on Spencer. I raised my hand.

"Let's let them finish, Hallie," Mr. Thompson said gently.

Spencer was really selling it. He made the game and the site sound way better and way cooler than Jaye and I ever could've. Bhavik shifted his weight from foot to foot, adding in a sentence about log-in names. I wondered if he knew that Spencer had stolen our idea.

"My uncle agreed to help us code the game," Spencer concluded. "So I promise, it will be next-level awesome."

And then, before Mr. T could say anything, Erica and Samara clapped. Actually put their hands together and made noise like Spencer was some kind of rock star or Steve Jobs.

I gave Spencer my best death glare.

The clapping shook Jaye out of her trance. She turned to stare at Erica and Samara. Why wasn't she calling Spencer out? He'd cheated. It was just like plagiarism!

"Hallie, did you have something to say?" Mr. T asked.

"Yes." My blood was boiling. "What he just—"

Jaye's hand clamped down around my wrist. Her fingertips pressed ice-cold against my skin. She shook her head urgently.

"Um, I—I—uh . . . ," I fumbled. She obviously didn't want me to expose him. But why? I was so confused. "Uh—nothing."

Jaye loosened her grip, her eyes darting about the room.

"Okay, then." Mr. T pointed to us. "Hallie and Jaye, the stage is yours."

Jaye didn't move. I didn't, either.

Now what? Were we really going to stand up and repeat the exact same idea? This was going to be a disaster!

CHAPTER 8
JAYE

How could he do this? Why would he do this? And to me? Why?

There had to be an explanation. Maybe it was a joke. But he wasn't laughing. No one was laughing.

It wasn't a joke.

I felt Hallie's eyes bore into me, heard Mr. Thompson's heavy footsteps heading toward us.

What do I do? Should I tell on Spencer?

I could. Hallie would back me up. But no one cared what the Bug Girl said, that was for sure. Owen and Raul weren't there when I'd told Spencer. And I was pretty sure no one had heard me telling him everything on the bus this morning and on the way into class. Everyone would definitely choose Spencer over me. Without Spencer, Erica wouldn't be my friend. Without Erica, Samara and Lily probably wouldn't sit with me at lunch. I was cool only because I was Spencer's friend. It had always been this way. Spencer made me important.

If I sold out Spencer, what happened to me?

"Everything okay?" Mr. Thompson's face loomed over our desks.

"Fine," Hallie said tightly. She nudged me, and I stumbled behind her to the front of the classroom.

Why had I gone and blabbed everything to Spencer? I was mad at myself and mad at him. He hadn't even wanted to be my partner. What gave him the right to pass off my idea as his?

I wished I were anywhere else. I couldn't look at Spencer.

Couldn't look at any of them. I stared at a black scuff mark across the toe of my left sneaker. It looked like a tidal wave.

What to do, what to do?

I could make a joke about both of us having the same idea. But I wasn't funny like that. Maybe we could *both* do a social media site?

I opened my mouth, but no sound came out. Everything swirled, and my stomach twisted in on itself.

And then Hallie was speaking. I tried to grasp the rapid-fire words coming out of her mouth. *What's she saying?*

Then a small groan escaped my lips.

Please, no. Not the bugs.

She was pitching her bug idea.

CHAPTER 9
HALLIE

I didn't have a choice.

Jaye was standing there like she'd been shot by a paralysis dart. So I did what my parents had taught me: Top a good idea with a better idea.

Eating bugs was a better idea. *Way* better.

And just like that, I started speaking. I didn't need any notes. I told how my mom stressed that I wasn't getting enough protein and how I'd had that light bulb moment when I ate the cricket on the field trip. I explained how people all over the world eat them. I explained that edible bugs solved a problem so much bigger than me not getting enough protein. It was global.

"Bugs are one of the most sustainable proteins on the planet. Eating bugs can reduce greenhouse gases, which cause climate change. Eating bugs saves water. Eating bugs can feed people who are starving because the land they live on isn't good for growing crops or raising animals." I was rattling off facts at a frenzied pace. "So that's why Jaye and I want to start a business that will sell bugs as food. We're going to change the way we eat—and save the world one bug at a time!"

I took a huge gulp of air. I'd been talking so fast that I'd forgotten to breathe.

"Whoa!" Mr. T flashed two thumbs-up. "That's a mighty impressive idea. I love the call to action. Jaye, anything to add?"

Jaye shook her head.

"That went well, don't you think?" I whispered as we walked back to our desks. I was especially proud of my "one bug at a time" line. I'd come up with it on the spot.

Jaye pressed her lips together, still not speaking. Her face was a weird pale color.

When the bell rang, I waited in my seat, expecting Jaye to finally tell Mr. T what went down. She could show him what she'd written last night to prove she'd had the idea first. Or better yet, just rip into Spencer. He so deserved it.

But she stayed slumped in her seat like a deflated balloon.

"Second-floor bathroom. Now." I dragged Jaye through the crowded hallway into the girls' bathroom on the second floor—the one that smells like rotten eggs, so we all avoided it. I peeked under every stall to make sure we were alone.

"What was *that*? We need to say something—" I began.

"I don't know . . . maybe he didn't mean—"

"Of course, he meant it—"

"You don't know him—"

"Do you?"

We spoke at the same time, our words tumbling over each other's. I took a deep breath and started again. "I'm sorry I went with the bug idea, but there wasn't anything else—"

"You totally saved us—"

"Yeah?"

"Yeah."

"Do you like it now?" I was bouncing on my toes.

"I didn't say that." Jaye's voice turned flat. "I don't know . . . I mean . . ." She dropped her head into her hands. "Why did he do that to me?"

Her hurt was so raw, I flinched. "Because he stinks and couldn't come up with his own good idea. And, hey, he did it to me, too," I pointed out. "We're partners."

Jaye raised her head, and I sensed something inside her shift slightly. "You're right."

"The bug idea is good, Jaye. Trust me," I said.

"I want to win." Her voice was hard and determined. "I want to crush Spencer and Bhavik. Pulverize them."

Her motivation wasn't pure, but so what? She was finally into it. I gave her a big hug. I'm a hugger, especially when I'm excited. "Come to my house this weekend for a bug hunt. First, we'll find the bugs. Then we'll eat them."

The weird paleness returned to her face.

CHAPTER 10
JAYE

I avoided Spencer for the rest of the day. It wasn't hard. He was avoiding me, too. And luckily, he didn't take the bus home that afternoon.

I was seeing him in a whole new way. A way that made me really upset and angry.

Ever since I could remember, Spencer had been full of himself, but that was part of his charm. And I knew a different side of him the other kids didn't see. Like the time his dog Slurpie died and he sobbed so hard, he threw up.

And the time when I had the flu, and he left a blue raspberry lollipop on my doorstep every day until I was better, because he knew I loved blue raspberry lollipops. Spencer could be a pain, but he'd never been cruel to me.

I didn't like the new Spencer. Not one bit.

I twirled a strand of my hair so tightly, I could feel my heartbeat in my finger. Nai Nai reached across the kitchen table and swatted my hand. She hated when I played with my hair.

Hallie would march across the street and demand an explanation, I found myself thinking. But Spencer was a master at talking his way out of trouble. He'd come up with some story or make me believe I'd told him it was okay to use our idea. Or worse . . . he'd tell me that he didn't like me anymore and that we were no longer friends.

Despite everything, I couldn't have him say that.

I saw Hallie again in my mind, opening her eyes really wide that way she does when she's trying to make a point.

I shook my head. It didn't matter what *Hallie* would do. Spencer and Erica were in a whole different social stratosphere. My friendship with them was way more complicated than she could ever grasp. She was too far out of the inner circle to begin to understand.

"The birds of worry are making nests in your hair." Nai Nai's concern reflected back at me through her black-framed glasses. "What is wrong? Tell me quietly."

Mrs. Chen was in the family room, tapping along to the metronome as Eddie ran through his B-flat scale. My cello lesson had been right before Eddie's. Mrs. Chen records our lessons so we can review her instructions as we practice during the week. If I spoke too loudly, I'd end up on the recording. It'd happened before.

"There's a girl at school who wants me to eat bugs. Actually, she wants the whole world to eat bugs," I whispered in Mandarin.

"Go on." Nai Nai stopped sorting snacks. She buys huge

boxes of crackers, then places exactly twelve crackers in little baggies for Eddie's and my lunches.

I explained about the pitch competition. I didn't mention anything about Spencer. "The idea won't work. No one *chooses* to eat a creepy-crawly bug."

"*I* ate them."

"What? You?" My grandma, who refused to try a taco or a panini at the mall food court, because she thought they wouldn't taste good, had eaten bugs? I stared at her in disbelief.

"The soil where I grew up was rocky, and crops were hard to grow. There were a few years when there was very little food to feed me and my brothers and sisters. The hunger pains were so strong, we'd wail throughout the night. But

we never starved. My mother understood that bugs gave nutrition. She boiled grasshoppers and made a steaming red ant soup that warmed our empty bellies." Nai Nai smiled at the memory. "She was a wise woman."

I gulped. It hurt to imagine my grandma, who loved to cook my favorite egg custard, as a hungry little girl. Suddenly I wondered how many kids were out there, hungry.

"Your family did what they had to do." I gently rubbed the back of Nai Nai's hand.

"No, no, Xiao Jie, you don't understand." She lifted my chin so I was gazing at her. "I *liked* the bugs. We all did. In China, they are also a delicacy enjoyed by the very rich. They pay a lot of money to dine on vinegar-soaked water bugs and roasted bee larvae."

"No way! I can't even." I rolled my eyes. "I mean, why? If I had mega-money, I'd order a large pizza."

Eddie's cello went silent in the other room.

"Add some ants or scorpions on your pizza. Now *that's* a

business idea—bug pizza!" Nai Nai chuckled, then stood to talk to Mrs. Chen.

"Do not mess with my pizza," I called after her. "Cheese and tomato sauce, that's it. There will be no bug-eating for me. I promise you that."

Two days later, on Saturday afternoon, Nai Nai, Eddie, and I sat in our car at the end of Hallie's driveway. She lived in the old section north of town, where narrow streets looped like a maze under a canopy of overgrown trees. The three of us stared in wonder at her mailbox. It was decoupaged with stamps from what I guessed were foreign countries. Who knew we were allowed to decorate mailboxes? All the ones on our street were plain black or silver.

"And there's other stuff down there." Eddie perched on his knees and pressed his seven-year-old face against the back seat window.

Sculptures lined the long driveway. Large twisted pieces of metal, spray-painted bright colors.

"Who is this girl?" Nai Nai asked suspiciously.

"Hallie's mom is an artist." I'd never seen sculptures on anyone's lawn. At the end of the gravel driveway, I spotted a small gray-weathered house. "I'll get out here." I didn't want a whole scene where I had to introduce Nai Nai and Eddie.

I hurried down the drive, staring up at the enormous sculptures. One had tiny bells hanging from it. Another had layers of rusty nails. One looked like a naked woman with a plastic beak and wire-mesh wings. I wasn't sure what they were supposed to mean.

Hallie wore olive-green pants with plaid patches sewn in at the knees and a tan canvas tool belt slung around her hips. It was bedazzled with rhinestones and stuffed with the strangest assortment of objects: a magnifying glass, little plastic cups with lids, a jar of bubbles, a jar of peanut butter, two goldfish nets, a black notebook, and a purple pen.

"Supplies," Hallie said, noticing me staring. "For our bug hunt."

"Riiiight." I followed her around the side of the house into an amazing garden filled with big-leafed plants and smaller metal sculptures. "Did your mom make all this art?"

"Yeah, they were done during her recycled-materials phase. She's moved on to ceramics. She's all about multidimensional expression."

"That's so cool." I didn't know anyone's parents who made art like this.

She handed me one of the little plastic cups. "You can put the bugs we find in here."

I pointed to the sticky label on the side. "Is this . . . is this from Dr. Stoddard's office?" Dr. Stoddard was my pediatrician. She had you pee into a little plastic cup so she could test for diseases or something. I was holding one of those little cups.

"You go there, too?" Hallie started through the garden,

and I hurried to catch up. "I asked Dr. S for it. Rubber gloves, throat swabs, too. They're great for art projects or science experiments. Don't freak out. It's a new one. Totally clean. Scoop up bugs with it and then we'll try 'em."

"Try them? But they'll be alive." I thought back to Nai Nai's story. "We need to cook them. Like in a soup."

"Bug soup! You're brilliant! We can do that!" Hallie pulled out the goldfish net. In one swift motion, she captured a black beetle crawling on a vine. "A little help here?"

I twisted the lid off the cup, and she plopped it inside.

"We need a lot more for soup." Hallie handed me the second goldfish net. She took the other cup. "It's a game. You should probably know that I'm always making up games. It's my thing. So for the game, we have five minutes to collect twenty bugs. I'll set a timer on my watch. Oh, and you have to yell 'Bug Off!' as loud as you can every time you get one."

Hallie nabbed a grasshopper from a leaf. "Bug Off!" When she yelled, she did a wiggle dance, as if she were a bee in a hive.

Hallie was funny.

"Get moving, Jaye. Clock's ticking!" she called.

I knelt and gently scooped three ants from between the paver stones. "Bug Off. Bug Off. Bug Off."

"Yell louder!" Hallie fished a water bug from a gurgling stone fountain. "Bug Off!"

"Bug Off! Bug Off!" I screamed as I trapped two more ants climbing up a chipped angel statue. It felt good to yell that loud. Soon we were both yelling, dancing, and laughing until our stomachs hurt.

"One more minute! Make it count!" Hallie called.

I reached for a spider clinging to a web, but Hallie stopped me, explaining how spiders were off-limits because they weren't actually bugs. We had eighteen bugs when her watch beeped, and we decided that was pretty excellent for our first time.

"To the kitchen for bug soup!" Hallie pushed open the back door.

Paintbrushes, a container of iridescent beads, old magazines, an assortment of springs, and wires littered the counter. Books on poetry and the battles of the Civil War were scattered, some bookmarked and some open, on the floor. An absurdly long lavender mohair scarf hung over a chair with knitting needles still attached. None of the chairs matched. A raggedy teddy bear wearing a crown of ivy and holding a spatula rested in the center of the wooden table. Initials and hearts were scratched into the table, as if it were still a tree.

Taking it all in, I felt dizzy. Anything was possible in this house.

Hallie filled a huge pot with water. She pulled three basil leaves off a plant on the windowsill and dropped them in. I dumped in the bugs, and together we watched them swim, pointing out our favorites. A few used the leaves as life rafts.

Hallie sprinkled in some pepper. I added some salt.

"Hey, Dad!" Hallie called out.

And just like that, her dad hurried in from some side room. He looked a lot like Hallie, except with a beard. Three yellow highlighters and a metal straw stuck out of the pocket of his red plaid shirt.

"Ah, this must be the partner in crime. Pleased to make your acquaintance." He raised his hand and gave me a jaunty salute. Then he winked. This time I shook it. "Quite a hive of activity here. You two look as busy as bees."

Hallie groaned at his puns. "We need to use the stove."

"The queen bee has spoken." He twisted the knob, and

the blue flame sprang to life under the pot. Hallie stirred with a big wooden spoon as the water heated up.

I stared at the floating beetles and ants. "This looks way gross. It needs noodles or something to make it soup, otherwise it's just bugs in seasoned water. And that's not going to fly."

"Jaye's punny!" Her dad flashed me a thumbs-up. "She fits right in."

I grinned, proud of my wordplay.

"So if we put in noodles, you'll eat it?" Hallie asked.

"Eat that? No way." I wrinkled my nose.

"Jaye's right." Her dad turned off the stove. "You can't eat random bugs you find outside. This soup could be dangerous."

"Hallie, I told you this whole thing won't work."

"It will so!" She planted her hands on her hips. "Fine, no soup. We'll come up with something else." Then she regarded me with the same suspicious look Nai Nai gives when she suspects I didn't brush my teeth, even though I say I did.

"I think anyone who's selling something should believe in it. We *are* selling bugs," Hallie declared. "And Mr. T says the judges ask us questions after the pitch. How can you answer them if you won't try our product?"

"You answer them." I shrugged. "Or I'll just make something up."

"That's lying." Hallie opened a cabinet and pulled out a small box that said *Crickets*. I recognized it from the school field trip. "These are good. Just eat one. Please."

"Uh . . . don't think so." I backed away.

"It's the *only* way we can win. Do you want to show up Spencer or not?"

Hallie knew exactly what to say.

Did I want to eat a bug? Heck no.

Did I want to win and show up Spencer? Most definitely.

If Spencer lost, he'd learn he can't go around stealing people's ideas. And maybe he'd go back to normal. And then we could go back to being friends. Winning would solve everything.

I opened the box and pinched a cricket gingerly between my forefinger and thumb. It was smaller than the chewable vitamin I ate each morning. But I couldn't tear my gaze away from the spindly legs.

"Uh-uh. Not happening."

"Watch me." Hallie ate one. "Come on, don't chicken out."

"I wish it were chicken." I grimaced.

"The crickets are fried and seasoned just like fried chicken," her dad put in, trying to help.

"Good to know." I stared at the little guy. "Okay, I got this . . ." I moved the cricket to my lips, but my teeth stayed clenched. No entrance allowed.

"Okay . . . okay . . . here I go." I tried again and again but still couldn't do it.

"I've got an idea." Hallie folded a yellow dishcloth, then

tied it around my head, making a blindfold. "It'll be easier if you can't see. Now open up."

I opened my mouth and tossed the cricket on my tongue, and before I knew it, I'd swallowed.

"I-JUST-ATE-A-BUG!"

"And?" Hallie asked.

I pushed up the blindfold. "Not bad. Too salty, but we can fix that."

"We can! Woo-hoo!" Hallie lifted my arm in victory. "Do you want another?"

"Don't push your luck." I laughed. "You know, we're going to have to sell a blindfold with each bug. It's the only way this is happening."

"It's not the only way." Hallie turned serious. "We just need to disguise them."

Hallie opened her notebook, and together we made a list.

Ways to Hide a Bug Menu

★ Bug cookies
★ Chocolate-covered bugs
★ Bug smoothies
★ Bug tacos
★ Bug sushi
★ Macaroni and bees

CHAPTER 11
HALLIE

"Your next assignment is to come up with a test product," Mr. T told us on Monday.

"What's that?" the whole class called out at pretty much the same time.

"A test product is a very simple version of your product," he said. "For example, Zach and Ava can cover bike helmets with different materials to see what works and looks best. You don't want to add in lots of details and special features now."

Jaye and I huddled together. Unlike a lot of the other teams, we needed a kitchen to make our test product.

"Come over to my house this afternoon," I said. "We can cook there."

"I can't," she said. "I have to practice cello after school."

On Tuesday, Jaye couldn't come over. On Wednesday, either. She always had to practice cello or take tennis lessons or play soccer or something. By Thursday, the other teams had already shared their test products in class.

Us? We had nothing!

My Top Secret Lowdown on the Competition!

Pitch Partners	Product/Service	Test Product
Me & Jaye	awesome edible bugs	Stay tuned! Coming Soon!
Spencer & Bhavik	social media app game (can you say, stolen?)	home page drawing (not totally horrible)
Erica & Lily	binder decorating kit	binder/sticker samples (dreamy scratch 'n sniff stickers!)
Samara & Jazmina	brownies with veggies	tasted like carrot cake, ok if that's your thing, but why not just buy a slice of carrot cake?

Raul & Peter	summer sled	computer drawing of sled & mini model (way cool!)
Owen & Vivi	online homework reviewer	video clip of them teaching geometry (lots of mumbling! great graphics!)
Sophia & Dion	sports jersey swap	list of swappable jerseys (I don't get this, but I don't wear jerseys)
Ava & Zach	personalized bike helmets	Design sketches—so cute, esp. the one that looks like graffiti!
Hunter & Luis	school lunch delivery service	sample menus (no way those restaurants will deliver—will they???)
Maddie & Noah	leashes for unusual pets (like squirrels!!!!!)	braided, beaded, and macrame leashes (lousy idea but leashes super nice)

Jaye kept saying she was too busy, and we needed to wait until the weekend. News flash: I stink at waiting. I'm absolutely horrible at it. Zara always gives me my birthday present a week before my birthday so I won't self-combust. I touched the beaded tassel hanging off my backpack that she'd made for my last birthday. I swallowed hard, pushing down a wave of loneliness, wishing desperately she were still here.

All week she hadn't answered my texts immediately like she used to. She said she was busy in her new school. Busy with her new friends.

Jaye was busy. Now Zara was busy, too.

After school, I went shopping by myself for ingredients.

I biked to the pet store where Henry buys bugs for Randall. There wasn't time for another bug hunt—plus my dad had said that backyard bugs aren't safe to eat. I read that it's because of fertilizers and insecticides and who knows what.

I handed the guy at the counter my list.

> 1 bag of crickets
> 1 bag of grasshoppers

Counter Guy wore an orange T-shirt that said *There Is No . Planet B*, so, naturally, he seemed like the perfect person to tell about our business, and of course, he was totally into it. A little too much, it turns out. He talked forever about climate change and how it was up to kids like me to fix the mess the adults had made. Finally, he handed me two small plastic containers with tiny holes in the lids. Tucking the containers into my wicker bike basket, I started up the hill toward home.

Then I changed my mind.

Counter Guy was so right. Our planet's in trouble—and that scares me. And makes me furious. Why should kids inherit this mess? But Jaye and I have a way to fix it. Eating bugs could help slow climate change, I was sure of it. The pitch competition was the first step. Once we won, we'd use the money to make it a real company and make real changes. I was on a mission to get bugs on everyone's plates! Who cared about cello practice? The time to save the world was *now*!

Like I told you. When I'm into something, I commit. Fully.

So instead of going home, I pedaled down the flat road that led into the east of town. If Jaye couldn't come to me, I'd go to her. That's what partners do.

"What're you doing here?" Jaye gave me a baffled look when she opened her front door.

I caught a snippet of a melody behind her. "Is that cello music?" I tried to peer inside. "How does that work? Does your cello play itself? You're standing here."

"Of course it doesn't. My brother's practicing. We take turns." Jaye furrowed her brow.

An old woman came up behind her. She asked a question in what I guessed was Chinese. Jaye answered in Chinese, and then they said some more stuff in Chinese. I was impressed. It was way cool that Jaye spoke another language.

"What're you saying?" I'd definitely heard my name.

"I told my grandma you came to do a school project. That's why you're here, right?" Jaye shook her head. "She wants you to come in. So weird. I usually can't have anyone over."

"Not even Spencer? Or Erica?"

"Well, yeah, him sometimes. I go over there mostly. And Erica . . . nah, that'd be too . . ." Jaye's voice trailed off as she searched for the right word.

I shrugged and stepped around her. I gave up on Erica back in fourth grade, the year she was especially mean to me.

"That girl's two-dimensional, Hallie, and we're three-D people in all things," my mom told me then. "You're too vibrant and creative. Do not live in her flat world."

I wondered if Jaye was actually two-dimensional, too. I sure hoped not.

"Hello." I reached out my hand to Jaye's grandma.

Her grandma eyed me up and down and shook my hand. She pointed to the two plastic containers, balanced one on top of the other. "What have you there?" She spoke English now.

"Hallie, you did not! Are those *bugs*?" Jaye cried.

"I got a bunch so we can experiment." I turned to Jaye's

grandma. "Any chance we can cook these in your kitchen? It's for homework. We won't make a mess, promise."

"Hallie, my house isn't like yours." Jaye spoke through clenched teeth. "Nai Nai, I'm sorry—"

"Hush." Her grandmother reached around Jaye and pulled me fully inside. "I like her. She sparks like a firecracker."

I grinned up at her grandma. "I'm going to be totally honest here. I can make scrambled eggs and soup from a can, but otherwise I don't really know how to cook." I added my sneakers to the line by the door, then scrunched my toes to hide the hole in my bright green sock. Jaye trailed after us into the kitchen.

I bet if I looked up the word *spotless* in the dictionary, the definition would be: *Jaye's kitchen*. It was absurdly spotless. No half-eaten muffins, no sticky spots of spilled juice, no signs of human activity whatsoever. I felt very out of place.

A small boy with spiky black hair wandered in. "Jaye

hasn't practiced cello yet. Who're you?"

"Mind your own beeswax, Eddie," Jaye said.

"Another bug pun! Score for you," I cheered.

"What? Oh, I wasn't trying to."

"Hi, kid, I'm Hallie." I squatted so I was eye level with Eddie. He had Jaye's same penetrating gaze. "Your sis and I are partners. We're professionals."

"Professional whats?" he asked.

"Bug chefs." I lifted the lid of one of the containers. A mass of pale green grasshoppers wriggled.

"Awesome," he breathed.

"Close that! They'll escape!" Jaye cried. "I can't believe you brought them in here."

"Believe it." I sealed the lid. "So I looked up how to cook bugs. We freeze them first. They're cold-blooded, so they'll just go to sleep and die in their sleep. Freezing kills them in the nicest way possible."

"Good to know." Jaye rolled her eyes.

"Can I put them in here?" I pointed to their freezer.

"Yes, yes." Nai Nai opened it and made room. I gave her a hug. She seemed surprised but went with it.

"You have Mrs. Stein, right?" I asked Jaye. We weren't in the same science class, but I'd remembered she was in my group on the field trip. I pulled my lab report from my backpack. "Want to finish this together while we wait for them to freeze?"

"Wait for them to *freeze*?" Jaye looked around in disbelief.

Nai Nai pointed to the table. "Yes, yes. Do your homework."

Jaye sighed, then found her lab report. We worked through it side by side. I couldn't believe how quickly Jaye puzzled out the answers. Homework with Zara took forever, requiring multiple study breaks. Jaye and I even finished our math problems, too. Eddie sat on my other side, stealing glances at me from under his long lashes.

"Bring a few grasshoppers to the stove, girls. Leave the

others in the freezer," Nai Nai said once we'd finished. She'd washed her hands and was tying a lavender apron around her waist.

"Yay!" I leaped up, eager to cook.

"Nai Nai, really?" Wonder filled Jaye's words.

"I have an idea. From back home." Her grandma looked as fireworks-on-the-Fourth-of-July excited as I felt. I almost hugged her again.

Nai Nai heated a splash of sesame oil in a deep, round-bottom silver pan. With quick, sure motions, she sliced green scallions, a carrot, a sweet red pepper, and a head of purple cabbage, dividing them into neat piles. Then she diced ginger and garlic. I'd never seen anyone chop so fast. I turned to Jaye. "She's our secret weapon."

"Are you making stir-fry in the wok?" Jaye watched her add the vegetables to the sizzling pan.

Nai Nai nodded. "A long time ago, when your father was a little boy, your grandfather and I took him to the night market in Beijing. It was his first visit to the city. Your father loved the crowds and the noise. We wandered through the market's busy stalls, the smells of the delicious snacks calling to us. We ended up sharing crispy stir-fried grasshoppers. The three of us. Together."

She dropped three grasshoppers into the pan. They popped as she doused them with soy sauce and sesame oil.

"I miss Ye Ye," Jaye said softly. Her grandma nodded. For a while, no one said anything, and we watched her grandma cook. A tangy-garlicky scent filled the kitchen.

"Nai Nai, it smells real good but"—Jaye pointed to the pan—"no one at Brookdale Middle's paying to eat this."

"Of course they will." Nai Nai waved her off.

"Our teacher says it's important to understand our customers. Kids like me, we don't want to eat bugs that look so . . . buggy. I mean, I can see legs and wings and things."

"I'll try it," I offered.

"Of course you will," Jaye muttered.

Nai Nai spooned some stir-fry into a shallow bowl. With Eddie peering over my shoulder, I scooped in a grasshopper along with a big helping of vegetables. It tasted like garlicky shrimp.

"So good!" I gave Nai Nai a double thumbs-up, and she beamed. Then I considered my bowl. "I think we need to do something easier to eat. Something you can hold in your hand. No forks."

"You can tuck the bugs inside spring rolls. Or jiaozi." Nai Nai began to slice more vegetables.

"I like spring rolls," I said.

"No." Jaye shook her head. "We should make cookies. Every kid loves those, and they're easy to eat."

"Fortune cookies! And inside is a live grasshopper!" Eddie whooped.

"That's beyond horrible." Jaye pretended to gag. "Chocolate chip cookies are the way to go."

"Don't you mean chocolate *chirp* cookies?" I asked.

"Look who's punny now." Jaye smirked.

Nai Nai cleaned up the stir-fry, setting aside the extra veggies for dinner, and I pulled up a cookie recipe on my phone. We grabbed bags of flour, white and brown sugar, baking soda, and a little bottle of vanilla from the pantry, then eggs, milk, and butter from the fridge. It was wild how organized their kitchen was. No way we'd ever find all this stuff at my house.

"First, we mix the wet ingredients. Then we mix the dry ingredients. Then we combine them," I said, reading the recipe.

"Are bugs wet or dry?" Eddie now stood on his tiptoes beside me. I liked having a little helper.

"Dry. We put them in at the end with the chips."

Jaye took over measuring everything out. As we mixed, I played tunes and made up a game that was like a dance. Three stirs, then spin in place three times and then pass the bowl to the next person. Eddie took turns, too. The object of the game was to pass it ten times before the song ended—or before one of us fell dizzy to the floor.

Flour flicked out of the bowl as we spun. Egg dripped onto the counter. Sugar sprinkled onto the floor. Eddie kept flopping onto his butt, and Nai Nai watched with an amused grin. From the way Jaye stared at her, I suspected her grandma wasn't usually cool about this kind of thing. But I have that effect on grown-ups. They think I'm charming or something. It's one of my weird superpowers.

"Bug time!" I plucked a bunch of crickets from the container in the freezer. They were the size of tiny peanuts, smaller than the ones Dr. Bugatti had given me. We folded them with the chocolate chips into the dough, scooped the cookies onto the baking tray, and pushed the tray into the hot oven.

And then we waited.

Jaye and I tried to out-pun each other. I'm ace at this, but she was surprisingly amazing, too. Nai Nai laughed, and we were having a grand ole time, until Eddie let out a blood-chilling scream that nearly gave me a heart attack.

"What?" I cried.

"They're alive!" He stood on a chair, his nose and palms pressed against the oven's glass window.

Jaye and I scrambled over. Nai Nai clapped her hand over her mouth.

"Oh. My. God. The cookies are *moving*!" Jaye pointed at the spreading mounds of dough, now wriggling and squirming.

"Hallie, what gives? You said freezing kills them!"

"It's supposed to." I was totally flustered. "Maybe twenty minutes isn't long enough in the freezer?"

"You think?" Jaye rolled her eyes.

"Take them out!" I screamed, suddenly horrified at cooking them alive.

"Are you nuts? They'll crawl everywhere," Jaye pointed. "Look!"

A cookie was inching its way past another cookie on the pan! It was as if the cookies had suddenly grown legs!

"Do it!" I cried.

Nai Nai was way ahead of us. She pulled on oven mitts and was sliding the mutant cookies out of the oven, when a loud *thud* and a gasp sounded behind us.

We all whirled around. Jaye and Eddie stiffened.

Their mom stood in the kitchen doorway, her hands

covering her mouth. Her heavy bag had dropped to the floor as she'd taken in the mess. Then her eyes landed on the squirming cookies. She was a tiny woman, yet in that moment she towered in the door frame.

She said something in Chinese, but I understood her perfectly.

We were in big trouble.

CHAPTER 12
JAYE

"What have you done here?"

Mama's voice was icier than our not-so-frozen crickets. It was super important to her to have everything in order in our house, in our drawers, everywhere. Now three kids, dusted with flour and sugar, were screaming in an epic mess-of-a-kitchen. And oh, yes, there were *bugs* escaping from half-baked cookies.

Eddie and I stood silent. I mean, what could we say? We had disappointed her.

But Hallie started talking. That girl is never quiet. In a tumble of words, she explained how we were trying to make a test product but didn't freeze the crickets long enough. She spit out a slew of facts about the benefits of eating bugs, gesturing wildly with her hands for emphasis. Even though Hallie can sometimes be strange, I was realizing she was supersmart. She knew stuff. Not textbook stuff like me. Or fashion blogger stuff like Erica. But important stuff about social issues and the world. And, of course, bugs. When Hallie gets going—wow!

Mama didn't react. It was as if she hadn't heard Hallie.

"Clean this up now." Mama spoke quietly to me and Eddie, then arched her eyebrows in Nai Nai's direction.

"I am sorry. You must go home now," she told Hallie.

My stomach knotted. Kids from school just don't belong here. Later, I knew, Mama would call Hallie "silly" or "not serious enough," like she always does with Spencer.

Mama left the kitchen, her footsteps climbing the stairs

to her bedroom. I was afraid to look at Hallie. She wouldn't understand.

"Hey, Jaye! Think fast!"

I raised my head and caught the sponge Hallie rocketed at me. She was humming that silly cleanup song they taught us in kindergarten and putting lids back on the baking soda and the vanilla.

"You don't have to do that," I said.

"I don't mind." She shrugged. "Yikes, that was *not* a good way for me to meet your mom, right? And I was psyched 'cause I've always wanted to meet a real scientist. You know, we could use a scientist's help. Isn't there something called food science?"

"I guess."

"Come to my house tomorrow. My parents are totally cool with us in our kitchen. And if we don't make *something*, we'll fail this part of the class."

"You will get a bad grade if you don't do this?" Nai Nai

abruptly shut off the sink faucet.

I nodded, and Nai Nai wiped her hands on a dishcloth and left the kitchen.

"Is she going up to Mama?" Eddie whispered.

This had gotten embarrassing enough. "Hallie, take your bugs and go. We got this."

"Really?" She gestured to Eddie. "Because it looks like he's giving your counter one of those body sugar scrubs!"

"Ugh!" My little brother had poured water on a pile of sugar and was swirling it around with a paper towel.

Nai Nai and Mama returned together to the kitchen, and Hallie said, "Hi, Mrs. W! I'm just helping clean up, then I'm biking home."

Mama nodded. "Thank you."

I don't know what Nai Nai said upstairs, but Mama looked more relaxed now. She even smiled. "Please, explain this school project to me."

Huh? I looked to Nai Nai. She pointed to the table with

her chin, where Mama had settled in. Hallie eagerly pulled up the chair next to her. I joined them, and together, we explained the pitch competition. Mama liked facts, but not in the jumble that had spilled out of Hallie's mouth earlier, so I tried to make it sound businesslike.

"Nothing is working," I finished.

Hallie jumped in. "We're kinda freaking out here, because all we've got are crawling cookies. We've never cooked bugs, so we're confused. My dad always says never be afraid to ask for help. You do experiments all the time, right? I think this is like that."

Mama considered Hallie with new interest. "It is too early for you to say nothing is working. In the lab, when an experiment fails, we approach it from a different direction."

"A different direction how? Do you cook?"

"No, but I do work with bugs." She told us about the tiny fruit flies she experimented on in her lab. Fruit flies have been part of many huge scientific discoveries with cancer and infections, because they're super easy to raise, only live for ten days, and share 70 percent of the same disease-causing genes as humans.

Turns out, my mother's quite the bug expert. Who knew?

"So any thoughts, Mrs. W?" Hallie asked.

"Approach it with logic, like a scientist. First list different ways to cook them," Mama said simply.

"On it." Hallie pulled her notebook from her purple backpack and began scribbling.

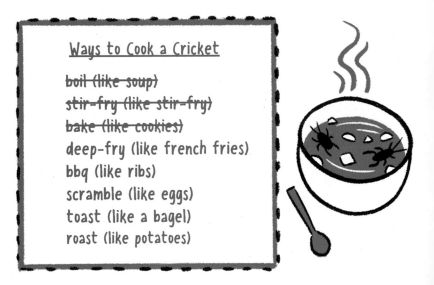

Ways to Cook a Cricket

~~boil (like soup)~~
~~stir-fry (like stir-fry)~~
~~bake (like cookies)~~
deep-fry (like french fries)
bbq (like ribs)
scramble (like eggs)
toast (like a bagel)
roast (like potatoes)

"Roasting." Mama pointed to that one. "It will dry them out. Make them easier to work with. First, our work space must be clean." She began to fold the sleeves of her navy blouse.

I eyed her suspiciously. My mother was motivated for worksheets and flashcards, but she didn't do school projects—that was Nai Nai's territory. I'd never seen her touch crayons or glue, and, for sure, she's never baked a cookie.

"You'll help? Woo-hoo!" Hallie cheered.

Mama nodded, and Nai Nai smiled approvingly. I could tell Nai Nai had pushed Mama into this—she was always pulling our family together. That's why I'm never letting her go back to China. What would happen then?

When the kitchen was gleaming, Mama heated the oven to a low temperature, and we took the crickets and grasshoppers from the freezer. They'd been in there for almost ninety minutes.

Hallie knocked one against the counter.

I breathed hot air on another.

Eddie stuck one under his armpit.

None moved. They were frozen solid this time.

We used the crickets, since they were smaller. We tossed them with olive oil and salt, then roasted them. After twenty minutes, Mama pulled the pan out and rested it on the stove top, and we carefully blotted away the extra oil with paper towels. The roasted crickets now looked like brittle, dried-out husks. Definitely way less buggy.

"While they cool," said Mama, "we must find a recipe to put them in."

Eddie hurried to pull a large cookbook with a shiny red-and-white cover from the bookshelf under the window. He raced back but was moving way too fast.

"Watch out!" I cried.

He thrust his hands forward to stop his body from slamming into the stove, and the heavy book launched into the air.

Thud! Crunch!

The cookbook landed with a *smack* onto the tray of roasted crickets.

"Are you kidding me, Eddie?" I lifted the book. Our bugs were pulverized.

"I'm sorry." His face crumpled.

"It's okay, kid." Hallie sighed.

But it wasn't okay. "Maybe it's a sign. The universe is telling us it's time to bail on the bugs and do something easier. Like a lemonade stand."

"Go ask Mr. T for another partner, 'cause I'm not bailing," Hallie shot back, clearly frustrated, too.

"Maybe I will."

"Fine."

"Fine."

I stared at Hallie. She stared at me. No way I'd blink first. I was the queen of staring contests. And the queen of stubborn. At least that's what Baba liked to say.

Wham!

Hallie and I both blinked.

Mama had smashed the cookbook onto the tray again.

"What're you doing?" we cried.

"Eddie fell into your answer." Mama raised the book. "Bug powder."

"Powder?" We moved closer.

"Crushing the roasted crickets makes a powder. See? A protein powder. You can easily mix it into other foods."

"Now the bugs are totally hidden. No more bug parts." Hallie grinned. "That's genius."

"You know what? Eating the whole bug is the deal breaker," I said. "I mean, no one eats a cow that looks like a cow. They eat hamburgers or meatloaf or steak. I can totally get behind this powder."

Who would have thought? My mother and my annoying little brother solved our problem!

The next day in class, during our Pitch Partner meeting, we told Mr. Thompson about our discovery.

"So is the cricket powder your product?" he asked.

"No. It's the main ingredient." I explained we hadn't yet cooked anything with it. "I'm thinking a granola bar. Or energy bar."

"Animal crackers! And we shape them to look like bugs!" Hallie declared.

"Animal crackers are, like, so third grade. Our product needs to be trendier," I insisted. "Maybe a krispie treat thingy?"

"Animal cookies are cute," Hallie said.

"Who cares about cute?" I sighed. Group projects were a whole lot easier with Spencer. He let me be in charge.

"Animal crackers are popular. Ask anyone."

"Exactly," said Mr. Thompson.

"Mr. T agrees with me!" Hallie crowed.

"No, I agreed with your idea to *ask anyone*," Mr. Thompson

said. "That's called market research. It's what companies do when they develop new products. Do a class survey. Let your customers have a say."

We typed out all of the choices on the classroom computer.

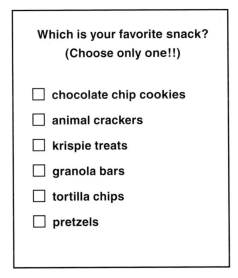

Which is your favorite snack?
(Choose only one!!)

☐ chocolate chip cookies
☐ animal crackers
☐ krispie treats
☐ granola bars
☐ tortilla chips
☐ pretzels

At the end of class, Hallie and I walked up and down the aisles, handing out our printed survey. I hesitated when I reached Spencer's desk.

We still hadn't spoken about what he'd done. I'd been pretending it hadn't happened and that I wasn't angry and that I didn't miss hanging out with him, which I knew was messed up because he'd totally betrayed me.

"Hey," Spencer said quietly.

"Hey."

"How's it going with Bug Girl?" He grinned, like we were sharing a joke.

"Fine." My voice came out strangely stiff. "Actually, great."

"Really?" He squinted up at me. "You're too cool to hang with *her*."

I felt myself exhale, even though I hadn't realized I was holding my breath. *He called me cool.* Maybe things were back to normal.

"Fill this out." Hallie appeared at my side and slapped a survey on Spencer's desk. Then she glued herself to me as if I were a turtle and she were my shell and guided me down the aisle until I was far across the classroom.

I kept sneaking looks at Spencer during class. But he wouldn't meet my eye.

That afternoon I left English class with Erica and Samara, and we walked outside toward the buses. They didn't realize anything was up between me and Spencer. He hadn't mentioned it, and neither did I. Erica was talking about the new sneakers she had seen at Sparks. They had stripes of mood-ring material running across them, and we debated how your feet know if you're happy or angry.

Then I saw Hallie waving at me. She stood by the big tree, bouncing on her toes that way she does when she's excited. Her feet most definitely know her mood!

I told Erica and Samara I needed to talk to my partner, and they understood. In the last two days, the competition had gone viral around the school. PITCH! posters lined the hallways, and Mr. Thompson had announced that parents were invited to watch us on our auditorium stage. My parents rarely came to school assemblies because of work, but I knew Nai Nai would be there.

Hallie showed me her notebook. "I tallied our surveys."

And the Winner Is . . .

- chocolate chip cookies   IIII
- animal crackers   II
- krispie treats   III
- granola bars   I
- tortilla chips   LHT II
- pretzels   III

"Market research has spoken. Slam dunk for tortilla chips," I said.

"Animal crackers were robbed." Hallie waved her arms above her head. "Hey there, Mrs. W!"

What? My mother never picked me up at school. But there was our small silver car idling behind the bus line.

"I took off early because it's Friday," she said when I

hurried over, as if this suddenly mattered. My parents work six days a week. To them, Friday was no different from Tuesday. "I was able to get crickets from the bug-supply place our lab uses. They will be safer to cook with than the ones from the pet store. And they are already frozen." She pointed to the blue insulated bag beside her.

I had rarely seen Mama this excited, her eyes so bright. And she'd left work! To do this project with me! Had Hallie put some sort of enchanted bug spell on my family?

I glanced at Erica, who was striding toward the buses, her long braid swinging. Then to Samara rummaging through her backpack.

"Get in!" I called to Hallie. "We've got chips to make!"

CHAPTER 13
HALLIE

 My Top Cricket-Cooking Tunes

* Any song by the Beatles
* "Lovebug" by Jonas Brothers
* "Fireflies" by Owl City
* "All My Friends Are Insects" by Weezer
* "Insects" by Oingo Boingo
* "The Cricket Song" by Rich O'Toole

Can we talk about the awesomeness of Mrs. W? When we got back to Jaye's house, she had the kitchen scrubbed down and disinfected. Each ingredient lined up. A list of instructions printed out. Nai Nai was out with Eddie at a tennis lesson. (The little dude's some kind of tennis star in the making!) She made me and Jaye wear aprons, and she even had these flowered shower caps for us to put over our hair. Jaye protested, but I wore mine proudly. There's nothing grosser than finding someone's hair in your food!

Mrs. W was totally chill about me pumping the tunes. She barely said anything, and Jaye was acting all quiet, and as much as I love to talk, tuneage was essential to fill all that empty air.

We roasted the frozen crickets like we did yesterday. Then we tucked them into a plastic bag and smashed them to smithereens with big, wooden mallets to make our cricket powder. I made up a game that was similar to one of those carnival games. Two points for every cricket demolished beyond recognition on the first *whack!*

Jaye won. I'm thinking she's either way strong or a bit angry—or both.

We mixed the cricket powder with corn flour and oil to form dough. After kneading it and flattening it with a rolling pin, we cut out little triangle shapes. Mrs. W fried them up carefully, one by one, in a pan of superhot oil. When my dad and mom cook, they're constantly tasting and adjusting, tossing in spices, turning up and down the heat. But, for our test kitchen, Mrs. W insisted we be both methodical and scientific.

We made several batches of chips. On some we sprinkled salt. On some we squeezed lime. On some we dusted cheese and on others, chili pepper. On some we did all four. Our rejects were piled high on the counters. Halfway through our seasoning explorations, Mrs. W disappeared upstairs to make a work phone call, but Jaye didn't seem to mind. She was too focused on getting the right combo.

It took all afternoon but finally, Jaye held up the winning chip. "This is it."

I agreed. "Applause for me. The bug-eating fraidy cat is

now a gourmet bug-eating chef!" I reached my hand over my shoulder to pat my back. "We'll conquer the world next!"

"First, we need to conquer our class." Jaye reminded me. "Have you met that group? They're harsh critics."

But I wasn't worried. "I have a plan for that."

On Monday, I squeezed onto the end of the long lunch table the girls' softball and basketball teams always claimed. Everyone shot me a side-eye. I didn't belong there, but I didn't care. Jaye's lunch table was right behind me, and that's where the action was.

It made zero sense to me why she continued to sit with Spencer, but, as she pointed out, why shouldn't she sit there? Her friends were his friends, and it wasn't like he owned the table.

Fair enough. Jaye could be friends with whoever she wanted. As long as it didn't mess up our business.

I strained my ears against the clanging of trays and chattering to listen in.

"Do you guys want some?" I heard Jaye offer tentatively. It'd taken a lot of convincing for me to get her to do this.

"Are those chips and guac?" Raul asked. "Gimme!"

"Yep. And the chips are homemade." Even though my back was to them, I knew Jaye had pulled out a big bag of chips and a container of my dad's special guacamole, just as we scripted.

"Who made 'em? Your grandma?" Spencer sounded suspicious. We'd expected this. No way he'd buy Nai Nai suddenly making Mexican food.

"I helped." Jaye turned to Erica. "Have you ever seen that bulletin the community center sends in the mail for old people? There are all these international cooking classes and pool yoga and other wacky stuff."

I silently cheered. Jaye had answered just as we'd planned. The two things she'd said weren't connected, yet it sounded like her grandma was taking a cooking class, which she wasn't. Best of all, neither was a lie.

I leaned into almost a full back bend to hear. Lily was babbling about a puppy-training class at the community center, but I was tuned in to the crunching and munching. Spencer, Raul, Erica, Samara, Owen, and Lily were chowing down on chips. *Our* chips!

Jaye totally surprised me with how calm she was playing it. She waited until only crumbs were left. "Whaddya think?

"Really good."

"Much better than store-bought."

"Those chips were dope! Do you have any more?"

As soon as Spencer asked that, I whirled around for a full-on view.

"Two, three, two, one, one, four." Jaye pointed at Erica, then Raul, then Samara, then Owen, then Lily, and finally Spencer as she counted off.

"What're you doing?" Samara asked.

"Counting the number of crickets."

"Where?" cried Lily, looking around wildly.

I stood, moving close to Jaye. "Oh, they're gone now. You ate them. In our delicious chips. There's about one cricket in each of our chips, so that's how many each of you ate. Thanks for your help. I'm thinking we have a winner."

"That was so unfair!" Erica cried.

"I can't believe I ate a bug," said Samara.

Owen shrugged. "I really liked them."

"Me too," mumbled Spencer. And I swear, he looked genuinely worried.

"Oh, so that's how it is?" Raul rubbed his hands together. "The competition's on. And I hope you know, I'm playing to win."

"So are we," Jaye and I said at the exact same time.

Later that day, Mr. T wrote on the whiteboard in his green marker: *PITCH! Countdown: 10 days!* Then he walked around the classroom for Pitch Partner check-ins.

Jaye watched Erica huddled with Lily. "Do you think they're angry with me for the chips?" she whispered as Lily cut a sideways glance at us.

"Nah, they're fine."

"I guess." She chewed her bottom lip, unconvinced.

"You were great," I whispered. "Did you see how Spencer's eyes *bugged* out? Our chips are certifiably good. We proved it."

When Mr. T reached us, I filled him in on our lunchtime taste-test success.

"I'd pump the brakes on that celebration," he warned. "People won't trust a company that tricked them. And if people don't trust your company, you'll fail. So how are you going to get people to *choose* to buy them?"

"More taste tests," I said.

"That's a good starting point. People spreading the word, telling their friends, sharing it on social media are also extremely powerful. But what happens if you can't do any of that?" he asked. "Let's pretend you're in the snacks section of a food store. The shelves are filled with chip choices. What makes you reach for a certain bag?"

"The name on the bag. And maybe the color of the bag. You know, if it catches my eye, I'd reach for it," I said.

"The description written on the bag, too," Jaye added. "If it sounds yummy."

"Exactly." Mr. T walked to the front of the classroom. "Business owners, listen here. Everyone needs a product name and logo. Did you know that before age three, most kids can recognize one hundred different logos?"

"That's messed up," said Lily. "They can't even read yet."

"It shows the power of an eye-catching logo." Mr. T said. "By your age, most of you recognize four hundred logos."

"We need a fantastic name," I said to Jaye. "How about Bug Bites?"

"That reminds me of being horribly itchy, and sticky pink mosquito lotion."

"Cricket Crunch?" I tried again.

"Ick. It makes me think of crunching the shiny hard shell."

"Six Legs Snacks?"

"I'm confused."

"Insects have six legs," I explained.

"Legs are a no-go," Jaye said.

"Well, I'm not hearing any ideas from you," I pointed out.

"How about Feed-the-World Chips? Or what about Sustainable Snacks?" Jaye offered.

I yawned. "Bo-o-o-ring. Too feel-goody."

We kept throwing out and rejecting ideas. Nothing sounded right. Mr. T suggested we play around with bug words.

"Okay, bug words. What do crickets do?" Jaye asked me.

"They fly. *Fly Chips*?"

"Or *Wing Chips*?"

"Crickets chirp," I said suddenly. *"Awesome Chirps?"*

"Chirps Chips," said Jaye.

"Chirps Chips! That's perfect!"

All week we worked on a logo.

Of course, we chose my mom's awesome logo.

By Friday, we had a name, a logo, and a fresh batch of chips that Nai Nai helped us cook, because Jaye's mom was at work. Now we just needed customers. Could we get random people to buy them?

We planned to meet tomorrow at two o'clock at Coffee Connection. We'd set up a table outside the coffee shop, just like the Girl Scouts do when they're selling cookies. Our goal was to sell twenty plastic baggies of chips.

Jaye said we'd sell out in an hour.

I said half an hour.

We were both wrong.

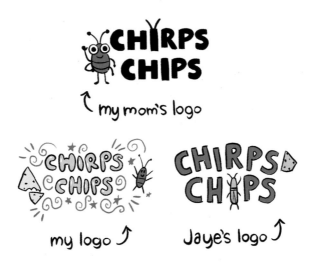

↖ my mom's logo

my logo ↑   Jaye's logo ↑

CHAPTER 14
JAYE

What were *they* doing here?

My breath caught in my throat as I peeked through the side window. I'd totally expected to see Hallie. I mean, who else would ring my doorbell *six times* at one o'clock on Saturday?

Erica and Samara stood on my front step, squinting up at my house.

"Who is it?" Nai Nai called from the kitchen.

"It's for me." I quickly opened the door. "Hey!"

Samara eyed my rainbow troll sweatshirt. Why hadn't they texted first? I so would've changed. I'd just come back from Saturday-morning Chinese school. I always wear my most comfy clothes there. But they were all dressed up.

I shoved the little origami turtle I'd just finished into my back pocket and stepped outside. "What're you up to?"

"Spencer lives there, right?" Erica looked across the street. "And you two are really good friends? Since like forever, right? That's what Lily told us."

I nodded.

"That's excellent!" Samara grabbed my hand.

"It is?" I had no idea what was going on.

"Raul texted us. He's at Spencer's now. They want us to come hang out. But it's weird, you know? Going over to a boy's house."

I didn't know. It'd never been weird to go to Spencer's house.

"If you come, Jaye, it could be like we were at your house

already and just decided to walk over. Real casual and all," explained Erica. "Isn't that brilliant?"

"So you'll come?" Samara asked.

"Right now?" I really, really didn't want to see Spencer. And besides, after lunch, I was going to ask Nai Nai to drop me at Coffee Connection. "I don't think—"

"It'll be more chill if you're there." Erica clasped her hands together, pleading. "We need you, Jaye. Please."

Erica Sanchez needed *me*. My mind whirled. If I did this, it would bond us. Like Krazy Glue–bond us. I swallowed hard, relieved to discover she wasn't angry that I tricked her with the chips. Everything between us was still okay. Better than okay.

I hurried inside and told Nai Nai I had to run to Spencer's for a quick school project. I knew by saying "school project," she'd let me go. Then I changed into my blue-and-purple flannel shirt.

Erica and Samara linked arms with me, and together we skipped to Spencer's. They made me ring the doorbell.

"Jaye! It's been so long. Where've you been?" Mrs. Montan crushed me in one of her squishy vanilla hugs. She has a thing for vanilla lotions and candles. Her hugs always leave me with a warm, happy feeling. But today, I felt awkward.

"There's a lot more homework in sixth grade." I was embarrassed to tell her about me and Spencer.

"Don't I know it? Spencer's dad and I have been on him to step it up. Grades count now." She gave me another squeeze, and we trailed her into the kitchen. "I keep telling him he needs to be more like you. So smart and serious."

Erica and Samara smirked, and my cheeks grew hot. Just then, Spencer and Raul slid open the glass back door. Spencer blinked rapidly when he spotted me. He does that when he's confused. We both studied our sneakers for a while.

In the backyard, Erica, Samara, and I hung on the side talking while Spencer and Raul kicked a soccer ball. But that got old real quick.

"Do something." Erica nudged me.

I suggested we play cornhole. Taking turns was tricky, since it was three against two. The whole time, Spencer and I avoided being on the same team. The weirdness was overwhelming.

After a while, I was the only one who cared about landing the beanbag in the hole. Spencer and Raul had moved on to mimicking kids at school. And Erica and Samara broke into fits of giggles at every unkind thing they said. And Spencer kept giving Erica this goofy grin.

That's when it hit me. This was a date thing. He *liked* liked Erica. I didn't belong here. I needed to go home.

"You've got to be kidding me!" Erica squealed suddenly. "What are *you* doing here?"

"Eww! She's spying on us!" Samara cried.

I turned to where they pointed. And saw Hallie peering over the wooden fence surrounding the yard.

"Get away, Bug Girl!" Spencer yelled. "This is my house. No one invited you!"

Hallie's eyes locked on mine for a painful moment.

And then I giggled.

It wasn't much, but it was enough for Spencer and Erica to join in. I slapped my hand over my mouth, but it was too late. Hallie's face drained of color at our combined laughter.

"No!" I cried. She had it wrong! I wasn't laughing at her. I giggle when I'm nervous. That's all it was. I started to explain, but the words didn't come fast enough. She bolted away.

My stomach twisted. "What time is it?" I hadn't brought my phone. "Someone, tell me!"

"Three," said Samara.

I'd promised to meet Hallie at two o'clock at the coffee shop. She must've been waiting this whole time, because the chips were in my house. And now she thought I was laughing at her!

I unlatched the gate and ran to the street just as a white car drove away from my house. Hallie's long chestnut curls blew out the window.

"Bye-bye, Bug Girl!" Spencer called in a singsong behind me.

And in that instant, the hot anger that had been brewing in my belly and that I'd pushed down all these weeks burst to the surface.

"Why do you have to be so horrible?" I cried. "You're all so mean!"

"Relax, Jaye." Spencer waved me off. "Just because Thompson stuck you with her doesn't mean you have to defend her."

I thought back to the bug hunt in her garden and our silly dance in my kitchen and all our puns. I'd had more fun with Hallie these past few weeks than I'd had with Spencer in months. I wasn't going to let Spencer bash Hallie. And I wouldn't bash her, either.

"You know what, Spence? Hallie is *way* cooler than you. We're creating something that's *so* much bigger than what you're doing. We're inventing a new food source. We're lessening humans' impact on the environment. Hallie is going to be like Malala but with climate change, like Greta, like . . . we're going to . . . to . . . to . . ."

I stopped sputtering. I was done wasting time with Spencer.

I needed to find Hallie.

CHAPTER 15
HALLIE

Top 3 Reasons I Miss Zara 💔

1. She never broke promises.
2. She never laughed at me.
3. She never was <u>MEAN</u>.

I refused to answer Jaye's flood of apology texts and voice mails. She'd left me holding my hand-lettered sign without any chips to sell, and when she didn't show up or answer any texts, I got worried that something bad had happened to Nai Nai, so I had my mom drive me to her house. But it turned out Nai Nai was fine. Eddie told me Jaye was across the street. And I saw her with them. Laughing.

Jaye had chosen Erica and Spencer over our project.

Erica was born awful, so that's no surprise, but I'd thought Jaye was different.

I'd thought she was nice.

I'd thought we were a team.

Partners.

Maybe even friends.

I'd thought wrong.

CHAPTER 16
JAYE

I folded dinosaur after dinosaur that night. It's the hardest origami animal I know. You have to keep flipping it over and over, then do tiny reverse folds and crimps. Making one takes forever, but I was fine with that. There was no way I was sleeping.

I kept replaying the scene in my mind. Kept hearing myself giggle. Kept seeing the hurt on Hallie's face.

I felt horrible. No, worse than horrible.

I'd been cruel, *and* I'd forgotten about testing our product, which was totally going to affect our grade and pretty much ruin our chances of winning. And tomorrow, I had to drive two hours to my auntie Lin's house for her fiftieth-birthday party. It was a huge family thing. She wasn't even a close relative, more of a second cousin or something. But that didn't matter. I had absolutely no chance of getting out of it.

The pitch competition was on Wednesday.

That left only two days. And we were in school most of the time. All the other teams had tried to sell their product. Not us.

I'd already sent Hallie a zillion texts and left five voice mails. She wouldn't reply. No surprise there. I'm sure she hated me now.

I should've had Nai Nai drive me to her house right away to apologize in person. But I'd been too embarrassed to tell Nai Nai how horrible I'd acted. I'd hidden in my room. And now it was way too late to go.

I understood why she wasn't speaking to me.

But I wished she would.

CHAPTER 17
HALLIE

The first cricket fell from my locker right after Spanish class on Monday.

It was small and green and made of paper. I scanned the crowded hall, wondering who'd tucked it into the slats of my locker. Was it a joke? Another way to make fun of me?

Tossing it into my locker, I slammed the door and hurried to science, making sure anyone watching saw they couldn't get to me. I didn't care.

But then another appeared. And another. After every

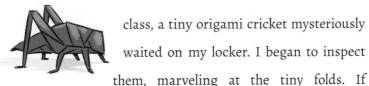 class, a tiny origami cricket mysteriously waited on my locker. I began to inspect them, marveling at the tiny folds. If someone was trying to mess with my head, they'd certainly taken a lot of time and care to do it. I was impressed, even though I didn't want to be.

Then right before BEE, a cricket holding a tiny toothpick "I'M SORRY" flag was on my locker. And I knew immediately who was leaving them.

I intercepted Jaye outside Mr. T's classroom and opened my hand, revealing five tiny green paper crickets. "They're amazing. If I could fold animals like that, I'd wear them in a chain around my neck or string them in garlands around my house."

Her face broke into a grin. "You're talking to me again?"

"Maybe." I stepped back to let a bunch of kids file through the door. The truth was I'd decided last night I'd talk to Jaye today. We needed to work together if we were going to win this pitch competition. I still didn't forgive her for laughing, but I wanted to win. Besides, I'm not big into holding grudges.

"I have a plan." We both said it at the same time.

"Me first. I was *so* stupid and horrible, and I'm *so* sorry. I never meant to hurt you," Jaye said. "I know we only have two days to write our pitch and test if people will buy the chips. I'm skipping cello practice and soccer practice. We'll go full force. Nai Nai promised to take us to Coffee Connection after school."

"Well, *my* plan was that I get the chips from you and sell them myself at the coffee place." I put the origami crickets safely in my pocket and crossed my arms over my chest.

Mom and I talked yesterday. She told me that sometimes not all partnerships are equal, and one person ends up being more passionate about the business. Obviously, that's me. I *know* our chips can make a difference. She said I had to keep taking the lead. I couldn't let Jaye bring me down.

"Oh . . . you want to do this alone?" Her voice caught.

"It's better, since you're always so busy. And you obviously don't care as much."

Jaye's cheeks turned red. "I care! A lot."

Yeah right, I thought. "You say that, but you've tried to get out of doing edible bugs a zillion times. Saturday was just one more time."

"That's not what happened," Jaye insisted. "Erica came over and—"

"I don't care about Erica. I care about Chirps."

"I do, too."

"Prove it." We were back to staring at each other.

"I won't mess up again. You'll see, Hallie." Jaye reached out her hand and grabbed mine and squeezed. *"I'm* giving you the Pitch Partner Power Pulse. It means I'm in one hundred percent."

I hesitated.

Jaye squeezed my hand again. "Partner promise."

I decided to give Jaye a second chance. She truly did seem sorry.

Besides, I'd always wanted a secret handshake.

"Maybe we can add a clap or a snap to the squeeze," I told her as we walked into class.

"Or go *buzz*," Jaye suggested. "And make antennae fingers."

"Punny!" I laughed.

And like that, we were back in business.

Cricket Math

You can figure out the temperature outside by how fast a cricket chirps!

1. Listen to a cricket & count # of chirps it makes in 1 minute.

2. Divide that number by 4.

3. Then add 40 to get the outside temperature.

(# chirps in 1 minute ÷ 4) + 40 = temperature outside

"No, no. You will get sick. You cannot go outside," Nai Nai argued with Jaye.

I peered out the rain-splattered window. Coffee Connection's parking lot was nearly empty on this cold, gray Monday afternoon. We'd tried begging the coffee-shop owner to let us sell our chips inside, but she'd refused. It had something to do with food safety, which I didn't get, because our chips are totally safe. She said the supermarket and the mall wouldn't let us sell inside, either.

"Maybe tomorrow will be better," I told Jaye.

"It won't be. The weather report is worse." Her back had gone all rigid. "We have to do this now."

Anyone who knows me knows I'm Plan A-All-the-Way. If my original idea hits a bump, I don't easily pivot to Plan B. But even I was ready to call today a washout. To my shock, it was Jaye who refused to give up.

She pulled Nai Nai over to the counter. There was a lot of whispering between them, and I saw Jaye's eyes tearing up, then there was more whispering.

I scooted closer to listen in. They spoke in both English and Chinese, intertwining the two. But I understood this: Jaye was telling Nai Nai the story of Spencer stealing our idea. And then she told how Erica had used her to get to Spencer. And, after some stuff I didn't understand, she said she really wanted to make things right between us.

They both glanced over at me, then Nai Nai tapped her watch. Jaye nodded eagerly and planted a big kiss on her cheek.

Jaye had convinced Nai Nai to let us do it!

EAT WHAT BUGS YOU!
CHIRPS CHIPS
$2.00 A BAG
MADE FROM CRICKETS!
SUSTAINABLE! HIGH PROTEIN!

Outside, we used extra tape to keep the sign from blowing off our small folding table. We lined up all the little baggies and held my unicorn umbrella over them.

"Want to buy some delicious chips?" I waved down everyone going in and out of the coffee shop. "Good-for-the-planet chips right here!"

People rushed past, too focused on getting their hot drink and racing back to their cars to stop. We tightened our raincoat hoods and offered chips to anyone who came near. Not many people did. The ink on the sign smeared. The baggies' cute little labels with our logo got soaked.

Nai Nai finally hurried outside. Our time was up, she said.

We'd sold only two bags of chips.

Both to Nai Nai.

Pure disaster.

"What's going on?" Henry strolled into the family room Tuesday afternoon and poked me under my arm. I hate it when he does that.

"We're practicing our pitch in front of the judges." I pointed to the stuffed animals lined up on the sofa—a floppy blue dog, an elephant in a plaid vest, and a pink cat whose ear I'd once crookedly sewn back on with green thread. "We've been recording it. Do you want to see?" I held out my phone.

"Nope." He flopped his large body onto the sofa, squishing the cat's tail under his leg. He pointed his finger at Jaye. "You're Jaye?"

She nodded and edged away. Last year Henry grew super tall, and with his broad shoulders, he now looked like this tough guy, but he was really a gentle giant.

"Let's keep working," I told Jaye.

We'd recorded ourselves practicing our pitch at least twenty times and analyzed every video. We fixed how awkwardly we stood. We figured out where to put our hands and how to make eye contact. Jaye was intense. She made us do it over and over. But now, with Henry in the room, she got quiet.

"You have five minutes." Henry kicked off his sneakers. "Hit me with what you've got."

"Really? Like do the whole pitch for you?"

"Four minutes and fifty seconds left. Ticktock."

I pulled Jaye next to me in front of the TV, and we read our lines from the note cards we'd made. When we finished, Henry was snoring!

I shoved him. "I know you're pretending."

He opened his eyes. "That was a snooze fest. Are you trying to bore the judges to death? You're spitting out too many numbers and percentages."

"The facts show why our product is important," I protested. "I researched them, and we emailed Dr. Bug at the zoo, and he gave us lots to use."

"I don't know who Dr. Bug is." Henry stood, then plucked the note cards from our hands. He riffled through, dividing them into two piles. "Every one of these facts prove crickets don't use as much water as cows. You don't need to give the percentage *and* show it in a pie chart *and* in a graph. It's fact overload."

"That's true." Jaye had found her voice. "Mr. Thompson said 'less is more.'"

"No, it's not. More is more, and less is less, so more is obviously better." I liked the facts. I wanted to keep them.

"That's dumb." Henry rolled his eyes. "You know what? Do your pitch without the cards."

"I can't. I haven't memorized it yet." Jaye and I had decided that I'd do the main part of the pitch, since she wasn't all that comfortable onstage. I reached for the cards.

Henry held them over his head. "You don't need them. You're not memorizing lines for a play."

I jumped, trying to grab the cards. But I couldn't reach.

"He's right. Mr. Thompson said to pitch like we're telling the judges a story," Jaye agreed.

With a satisfied smirk, Henry flopped back onto the sofa, still holding the cards.

"Hallie, no one knows more about these chips than you," Jaye said, seeing me frown. "Can't you just talk?"

Of course I could talk!

I took a deep breath and told the story of how my mom wanted me to eat more protein, and we were worried about climate change, and with these chips, we felt we had a way to make the future brighter. Jaye cheered when I finished, but Henry tilted his head. "It's a lot better, yeah. But it's missing a wow factor. You should add something bold, make a—"

"Make a statement," I finished. He was right. We needed a wow factor.

"Wake those judges up. If it were me, I'd do something wild at the beginning," he said.

"Wild how?" For Henry, that could mean anything. He once wore a pirate costume to school for a full week. It wasn't for a school project, and it wasn't Halloween. Henry did it to protest music piracy. He wanted to make kids aware that downloading free music from sketchy sites hurts the musicians. Henry is also all about making a statement.

"I'd build a huge, mechanical, remote-controlled cricket and have it walk onto the stage." He clicked on the TV. *Jeopardy!* blared from the screen.

Jaye showed me her phone. Nai Nai had already texted twice that it was time to leave.

"I love the robot cricket idea," I told Jaye excitedly as we walked toward the front door.

"We can't build a robot. Especially by tomorrow."

Jaye was so annoyingly practical.

"Okay, so not that. But something else. Maybe a poem or a dance? We need to get the judges' attention so they—"

"Our pitch is good, Hallie."

"Not good enough," I insisted, my hand now on the doorknob. "We need to do something totally unexpected or"—and in that instant, I knew what to do—"something totally expected."

I loved my wacky idea. It was so *me*. And even a little bit Jaye.

"No way! Absolutely not!" Jaye freaked out when I told her. "It's so weird."

"Weird is good."

"People will laugh . . . the judges will laugh."

"That's the whole point." I wished Jaye weren't so scared to stand out.

"It won't help us win. Don't do it," Jaye warned, getting

into Nai Nai's waiting car.

"Fine." I didn't feel like arguing. I waved to Nai Nai.

Jaye arched her eyebrows. "Seriously, Hallie. What we have is great. Just do that, okay?"

"I said fine."

They drove off, and for a moment, I truly considered not doing it. But I really, really wanted to.

So I texted Zara.

Since she moved, days passed before she answered my texts. It probably had to do with being so far away. Or having new friends.

I couldn't believe it! She texted back right away.

Zara said my idea was amazing, just like I knew she would. It was a risky move, sure, but we agreed these chips were urgent to the health of our planet. I *had* to do it.

Besides, I figured Jaye owed me.

CHAPTER 18
JAYE

Backstage was sweltering, even though it was late October. I scratched underneath the collar of my stiff white blouse. Nai Nai made me wear it, along with a knee-length navy wool skirt. I pointed out that I looked like the woman who worked in the bank, but Nai Nai said I looked professional. All the other families must visit the same bank, because backstage was a sea of uncomfortable sixth-graders in navy, white, and khaki.

I could hear the other teams practicing their pitches

in whispers. My stomach churned. It felt as if that whole container of frozen grasshoppers had come alive inside me.

When Mr. Thompson learned we'd gotten rained out, he said these were "early days" in the development of our product, and if we made it to the next round of the competition, we'd have plenty of time to sell our chips and improve our business plan.

But that meant we had to win.

And that meant I needed Hallie.

Where was she? She was the only one not here.

I scanned backstage, knowing she'd be easy to spot. I couldn't imagine Hallie's parents making her wear a navy skirt. Hallie didn't do plain. My eyes widened when I saw her.

Not Hallie. My mother peeking in the backstage door.

"Is Nai Nai okay?" I hurried over.

"Fine. Fine." She smoothed my staticky hair with her hands. "I switched my schedule. Baba wanted to come, but he had to give a paper at a conference."

"But you never come to my school things," I said, confused.

"You worked hard. I would like to see you and Hallie up there. Building a business takes courage. I am proud you are learning this." Mama stared at me, as if seeing me for the first time. "I am proud of you."

I felt my cheeks go warm. I gave her a huge smile. It's as close to a hug as my family does. My mind raced ahead, searching for ways to stretch out this moment. "But I don't have courage. I'm really scared right now."

"You do not need to be scared. We have a deep pool of courage." She tapped my chest. "It is there, inside you."

I didn't say anything. She didn't know about that fluttery feeling I got in my stomach.

But this time, Mama filled our silence. "I have been scared many times."

"You?" Mama always seemed so calm and sure of herself.

"I was very scared when I chose to leave my home and

to leave you. I was very scared to go across the world to an unknown place."

"But you had Baba. You came together," I pointed out.

"He did not want to go."

"What?" I didn't know this.

She shook her head. "It was my idea. I hoped if we came and worked hard, life would be better. You would learn things like you are learning now. Your Baba wasn't happy in China, but he was comfortable there. He does not like change."

"So what happened?" I asked eagerly. Mama had never shared stories about her life.

"I had to draw on my inner pool of courage for both of us and push him to go." A quick shadow crossed her face, then disappeared. "You are like me. You have courage."

"I think I might be more like Baba. I don't like change." I swallowed hard, thinking of Spencer and starting middle school.

Mama tenderly touched my cheek, taking me by surprise.

She was about to say something, when everyone backstage erupted into laughter.

What was going on? I stood on my tiptoes—and gasped.

A life-size, bright green cricket with black fuzzy antennae and white Styrofoam eyes was walking toward me. And calling my name. And waving.

Hallie! In a homemade cricket costume!

"Bug Girl, reporting in," she said, giving me a mock salute.

"Oh, no, you didn't." I squeezed my eyes shut. Maybe if I didn't see this, no one else would. The bad, fluttery feeling in my stomach got worse.

"Go big or go home, right? Do you like it? My mom helped me make it."

I opened my eyes. "You *said* you wouldn't do it. That's not fair."

Her grin faded for once. "I know. But Zara and I were talking last night, and she thought it was a cool idea and—"

"Zara? Zara isn't part of this," I snapped. "She's gone."

Hallie flinched as if I'd slapped her.

I gulped, wishing I hadn't said that. I knew from all her stories how much she missed her. I tried again. "It's you and me now. We're business partners." I was about to add "and friends" but felt myself hesitate and then felt awkward for hesitating, so I didn't.

"I asked Zara because you always say no to my ideas. You don't listen to me."

Suddenly I felt my mother's hand resting on my shoulder. I'd momentarily forgotten she was there. Her other hand was on Hallie's shoulder. She shook her head, unhappy we were arguing. "This is not good, girls. Not now."

I gulped. Mama had come today to see me. She'd said

she was proud of me. I didn't want to upset her. And I really didn't want to be mad at Hallie, either.

"I'm sorry. I'll try to listen more," I told Hallie. I hoped she knew I meant it.

"I'm sorry, too. Sometimes I get so into something and . . . well . . ."

I giggled, then cringed. "I do that, you know, when I'm nervous. Giggle. It doesn't mean anything."

Hallie's eyes widened, and I think she understood.

Then Mama brought our hands together, resting my palm in Hallie's. She patted our hands wished us luck, and left to find her seat next to Nai Nai.

"Jaye, I'm okay with taking off the costume." With her free hand, Hallie started to lift her headpiece.

I heard snickers behind us, but this time I didn't turn to see who it was. I was finally looking at Hallie. At her puffy green body. Her giant antennae. Before I could stop myself, I was giggling. Not to make fun of her, but the opposite.

"It's un-*bee*-lievable!" I reached up to thwack the wobbly antennae.

Hallie was so brave and silly and willing to do anything to make these chips work. And in that moment, standing next to her in that cricket costume, I felt brave, too. "Definitely keep it on. I was wrong. I like it!"

"Really? I knew you had some weird in you, Jaye Wu!" She raised her hand for a fist bump.

I leaned in and bumped it. "That's why we're friends."

"Yeah?" Hallie held my gaze.

"Yeah." I grinned, realizing how right it felt.

"We are!" Hallie beamed. "Let's do this, Bug Girl."

We joined the other teams, lining up in the order we'd present onstage. Hallie and I were second. I was curious to watch the others. In class, Mr. Thompson had had each team practice privately for him so we wouldn't be influenced by other pitches.

As we huddled together to run through our pitch one last

time, I noticed Spencer and Bhavik talking to Mr. Thompson off to the side. They both looked upset. Then Bhavik stalked off, and Mr. Thompson hurried after him. Spencer slumped against a plastic potted plant once used for the school musical. He buried his head in his hands, and his shoulders shook.

No one was paying attention. After a while, I couldn't help myself. I went over to him. "Are you okay?"

He didn't look up. "Everything fell apart, and Bhavik's mad. I think I'm in trouble."

I squatted down. "What happened?"

"I've been promising Bhavik that Uncle Gabe was working on a prototype for the game, building a site for us, that everything was under control."

"And he wasn't?'

He shook his head. "I didn't get to ask him until this week, because he's been away. He said he'd help out, but then he was called into a big project. I just assumed he'd be all over it—I was so positive he'd buy the company from me and Bhavik, and we'd cash out big-time. So I kind of let Mr. Thompson and Bhavik believe Uncle Gabe was doing it all this time."

"But what about the progress reports?" Each team had to submit weekly reports to Mr. Thompson with examples of what was working and what wasn't. They would've had to show a prototype of how the game worked.

"I might have made some stuff up. And used stuff I got from other sites." Spencer raised his head, and his eyes were wet. "Bhavik won't go onstage, because he says our pitch is a lie. Mr. Thompson is telling my parents and the principal."

I stared at him, unbelieving. "That's messed up, Spence."

"Yeah." He studied his shiny black shoes as we both contemplated how much trouble he'd get in.

"Why'd you do it?" I finally asked in a low voice.

I wasn't asking about the progress reports, and he knew that.

"I'm sorry. I didn't plan it." He sighed. "It's just that your project sounded so cool. I told Bhavik about it before class that day. Bhavik thought I'd come up with it. He loved it, so I just kind of went with it. Besides, you didn't have anyone to code it, and I had Uncle Gabe, so it seemed to make sense . . . I don't know . . . Before I knew it, I was pitching it. I felt bad afterward."

"If you felt so bad, why didn't you ever own up to it?"

"I wanted to. I wrote an email to Mr. Thompson, but I was too scared to send it. And by then we'd added a lot to it, so it felt like ours. And you and Hallie were killing it with your chips, and you seemed happy about that." He bit his chapped lip. "I'm sorry."

"Okay." I nodded, accepting his apology. But I couldn't think of anything to say that would untangle his web of lies. I was sad that I didn't like him as much anymore.

"Jaye! Jaye! They're starting!" Hallie called.

I left Spencer and hurried to join her. We peeked

through the small opening in the velvet curtain. The lights had dimmed, and Mr. Thompson was introducing the three judges to the audience.

"We are honored to have Mayor Kari Godfrey, local business owner Victor Samuels of Samuels Cleaning Solutions, and Nina Apolito, president of the chamber of commerce, join us today." He gestured to the front row of the audience, where the three adults sat in a line.

"Each team will have exactly two minutes to pitch." Now he gestured to a big timer set up on the stage: 2:00 blinked on the screen. "At the end of two minutes, we will cut them off. So watch your timing, teams!"

Sophia and Dion were first up and positioned themselves in front of the two side-by-side microphones. Each wore a different sports jersey. As soon as Dion greeted the judges, the red numbers on the clock began counting down.

They explained how passionate sports fans wear gear to show team love, but jerseys are expensive, especially when you follow football, baseball, *and* basketball teams. Their jersey-swap site would showcase everyone's jerseys and make trades easy. Trades could be permanent or for a short period of time. They displayed graphs of research they did in school and around town, and it seemed people were excited.

Then they stripped off their jerseys to reveal a different jersey underneath, which was clever, except Sophia's gold hair clip got caught, and she struggled to pull the first jersey over her head. Dion was unsure if he should help out, so he stopped speaking, and then the timer buzzed.

They never got to finish. I felt my legs tremble. What if that happened to us?

"Next up is Chirps Chips," Mr. Thompson announced into the microphone. "This team has an innovative new food product that gives meaning to the expression 'Eat what bugs you.'"

This was it!

Hallie looked at me. "Ready?"

I nodded tentatively.

She raised her eyebrows.

I made myself take a deep breath and square my shoulders. "Yes!"

Hallie and I grabbed hands and squeezed at the same time. Pitch Partner Power Pulse.

Then we jogged onto the stage.

CHAPTER 19
HALLIE

I let the audience's laughter roll over me as I waved to the crowd. Squinting into the bright lights, I scanned the judges' faces. Fear and excitement rippled through my body. Yes! They were grinning, just as I'd hoped. But come on, who wouldn't smile at a huge cricket?

Then I got serious and we began our pitch.

"Hi, everyone! My name is Hallie, and this is Jaye, and our product is Chirps Chips, a chip made from cricket powder."

"Crickets? For real?" Jaye asked, just as we'd rehearsed.

"You know it! Edible bugs are good for you and good for our planet. In 2050, Earth's population will increase to almost ten billion people. Right now, the animals we eat use up fifty percent of the fresh water in America. How will we feed everyone without destroying the environment?"

"Luckily, we have the tiny cricket," Jaye added.

"Raising bugs takes way less energy and resources than raising animals or growing crops," I continued. "It takes one gallon of water to make one pound of crickets. But to produce one pound of beef, it takes two *thousand* gallons of water. Eating a Quarter Pounder is like showering for an hour and a half! Plus you can farm crickets in a small space, so you don't use all that land."

"But do bugs taste good?" Jaye asked.

"Most of the world thinks so. People in eighty percent of all countries already eat them." I pointed to a map where we'd highlighted these countries, then I looked directly at the judges. "But we discovered that convincing our friends to eat a whole bug was tricky."

"So we experimented a lot and created our own cricket powder and baked it into our most favorite snack food— chips. Our chips are delicious and nutritious"—Jaye held up one finger—"and there's one cricket baked into every chip. Crickets are full of protein, vitamins, and minerals."

I glanced at the big clock. Ten seconds left. We had to hurry!

"We hope you will invest in our business, so"—I raised a big sign that read "EAT BUGS!"—"we can save the world one bug at a time! Bug appétit!"

Then Jaye leaned over the edge of the stage and handed each judge a little baggie of our chips. My heart was racing. Had I gotten everything in? Had I spoken too fast?

"Your chips are good," Mayor Godfrey said after eating one. "Tell us about how they're made."

Jaye gave a short explanation, without giving away our top secret recipe. We were super careful now about people copying us! She also showed our packaging and logo. Mayor Godfrey scribbled something on her pad of paper. What was she writing?

Then Mr. Samuels asked where we planned to sell the chips.

"We'd like to get them in both the snack aisle and the healthy-food aisle of grocery stores," I said. "But first, we're going to try to sell them at school events and sports meets to build brand awareness."

I grinned over at Mr. T, proud I'd managed to use one of the business words he taught us.

"Tell me about the consumer response to your chips." Mr. Samuels leaned forward.

Jaye tensed up beside me, but we'd decided yesterday we'd own up to it.

"We haven't tested them outside of school," I admitted. I explained that the next step in building our company would be proper testing to be sure we were baking a product that consumers wanted.

"How would you use the prize money to grow your business?" Ms. Apolito asked. She'd asked Sophia and Dion this same question.

Jaye was ready. "We'd use the money to buy crickets to make a lot more chips. We'd also use it to cook in a professional kitchen. My mom wasn't so happy about our kitchen swarming with bugs!"

The audience chuckled, and I heard some cheers, but that might have been my dad. And then Mr. T motioned us off the stage and called Raul and Peter on.

"Do you think it was good?" Jaye whispered as soon as we were hidden behind the curtain.

"No," I said, looking serious for a moment. "I think it was pure awesomeness!"

"Me too!"

We jumped up and down until Mrs. Stein, who was helping backstage, shushed us. I quickly changed out of my costume, and we found seats to watch the rest of the pitches. By the time the last team finished, our entire class was sitting together in the front section of the audience.

I stared at the backs of the judges' heads as they leaned together, deliberating. What was there to talk about? It seemed fairly obvious to me.

Why Chirps Chips Deserves to Win

1. We were THE BEST
2. Only team in a costume
3. Only team changing the world

Finally, Mr. T returned to the microphone. He gave a long speech about how we were all winners. Maybe, but only one team was going home with the prize. My leg jiggled with anticipation.

"In third place," he began, "we have Design and Decorate, with their custom binder kit."

Erica and Lily hurried onto the stage, and I squeezed Jaye's hand. We weren't in third. All signs pointed to first. A nervous shiver shot through me.

"And in second place, Chirps Chips!"

That had to be a mistake! We were too good for second place.

Jaye nudged me out of my seat. My heart felt like it had fallen into my stomach. Together we climbed the stairs onto the stage. The audience cheered, and I spotted my parents clapping wildly, so I forced a smile. I didn't want anyone to think I was a sore loser.

"Now for our winner . . . with the innovative summer

sled, Team Summer Sled!"

"Woot-woot!" Raul bellowed as he and Peter leaped onto the stage. Mr. T handed them the oversized check. The six of us stood in a line as the audience applauded, and parents took pictures. I spotted Nai Nai recording us on her phone, and Mrs. W was looking at Jaye and tapping her finger to her chest for some reason. Jaye beamed back at her mom.

"Second's not terrible," Jaye said, glancing at me as we exited backstage.

I sighed. "I know, and their sled did look fun. And it's cool that they're donating money to save the polar bears for every sled sold."

"Not testing the chips hurt us. I'm sorry." Raul and Peter had shown videos of kids riding their sled in the park and giving enthusiastic reviews.

"It's fine. Finding the right recipe took a long time—"

"So did figuring out how to work together," Jaye added.

I agreed. "What *bugs* me is, compared to the others, our

chips stand for something, you know?"

"We should still make the chips and sell them," Jaye said. "Just because the mayor and a cleaning-supplies guy didn't pick us doesn't mean we should stop. I have birthday money we can use and—*whoa!*"

I wrapped my arms around her in an impulsive hug. Hearing she didn't want to quit and knowing that we were really and truly friends, well, it made me spontaneously happy, even if we hadn't won.

"Okay, I guess we're hugging." Jaye giggled and hugged me back.

Like I said earlier, eating bugs can change your life.

"Excuse me! Pitch winners, come here." A young woman with dark hair in a messy bun and cat-eye glasses waved us over. "I'm with the *Brookdale Times-Courier*. I'd like to take your picture and ask a question or two for an article."

"We're going to be in the paper?" I asked, letting go of Jaye. I'd never been in a newspaper before.

The woman nodded. "And I want *you* front and center. That costume was brilliant. Can you put it back on?"

You know it! I quickly transformed back into Bug Girl.

The reporter pulled out her phone and positioned us, with me in the middle. "Okay, everyone say—"

"Bugs!" I cried.

She snapped several photos. Then she asked Raul and Peter some questions. They said how proud they were to win. Peter gave a big shout-out to Mr. T, which I thought was super nice.

"Now, girls." She turned to us. "What are your plans to prepare for the countywide competition?"

"Wrong team," I said.

"Yeah, they came in *second*. We move on to that," Raul put in.

"The Eat Bugs girls do, too. The rules state that the top two teams from each school move on," the reporter announced confidently.

Jaye and I ran to find Mr. T and had the reporter repeat what she'd told us.

"Is she right?" I demanded.

"I don't think so . . ." He pulled up the rules on his phone and scrolled through. "Well, hold on . . . hmmm . . . oh . . ." He looked at us sheepishly. "Somehow I missed that. It's buried here. The top two teams do go on. But I'm sorry to say only Raul and Peter win the money—"

"Woo-hoo!" I jumped up and down. I didn't care about the money. Jaye and I would be able to keep Chirps alive!

CHAPTER 20
JAYE

Two weeks later, I stood in front of the classroom, trying desperately to get everyone's attention. I cleared my throat a bunch of times, but no one listened.

Finally, Mr. Thompson let out a sharp whistle, coming to my rescue. "Quiet down, folks. Jaye's about to call the first meeting of the Pitch Club to order."

"Hi there." My voice shook. Why did I let Hallie talk me into being club president? She said I'm a lot more organized, which is true, but she'd be so much better at standing up here. I wasn't used to being front and center.

I couldn't believe how many kids had shown up. Twenty faces looked expectantly at me. I recognized a bunch—Raul, Erica, Samara, Owen, Lily—but there were some I'd never seen before. Spencer—no surprise—was not here.

Hallie sat in the front row. She was hard to miss in her green antennae headband. She wore it all the time now. She shook her head, making the antennae wiggle and me giggle.

"Right after the pitch competition, before we knew we'd made the county competition, Hallie and I talked about how much we wanted to continue building our business. That's how we came up with the idea for an entrepreneur club," I began. "This club is for kids from BEE who still want to work on their startups and for anyone who wants to develop one. Mr. Thompson agreed to be our club adviser, but there are no grades or homework. It's for fun. Just a place to work together."

I finished by explaining we'd meet every Thursday after school. (Nai Nai had moved my tennis lesson to Friday.)

Then Mr. Thompson jumped in. "Push yourself to think creatively and take risks. We're looking for out-of-the-box ideas in this club. Okay, let's start by breaking into teams."

"We have a lot of things to fix and make better," I said as Hallie and I pulled two desks together. "Number one is—"

"Don't have to number them. Just spit 'em out randomly." She opened her notebook.

"But that's just it, Hals. We can't be random about this. We're in the county competition now. That's huge. We need a real business plan."

"Excuse me, Mr. Thompson?" Ms. Stallings, the school secretary, pushed open the classroom door with her suede boot. In her arms, she carried a large brown box.

Mr. Thompson hurried over and tilted his head as he

read the label. "Hallie? You had something sent to the school care of me?"

"It's here!" She ran over.

"What is it?" Ms. Stallings asked as Mr. Thompson pried off the tape.

"Crickets," said Hallie.

"Excuse me?" Mr. Thompson had already lifted one flap. "You sent them *here*?"

"I found an excellent cricket farm online. My dad helped me talk to the guy, and when he heard about our chips, he agreed to send the first batch for free. Isn't that great? I knew we were having this meeting, so I said he could overnight them to the school. Jaye and I have *a lot* of chips to make."

Mr. Thompson stared at the ceiling for a moment, his hand hovering over the second flap. "Dare I ask how many crickets we're talking about?"

By now, all the club members had gathered around. Even Erica and Samara.

Hallie shrugged. "Five hundred. Or so."

Mr. Thompson's eyebrows shot up into his forehead.

"Come on, Mr. Thompson." I hurried to Hallie's side. "Didn't you just tell us to think *outside the box*?"

He smirked. "You got me. I did."

"Open it. Let's see the bugs," urged Owen, and the rest of the club cheered.

Mr. Thompson slid the box toward us. Together Hallie and I pulled back the flaps—and I lifted out our new batch of crickets.

EAT BUGS WAS INSPIRED BY A TRUE STORY.

Laura D'Asaro and Rose Wang, cofounders of the *real* Chirps, were roommates at Harvard University. While studying one summer in Tanzania, Laura (an off-and-on vegetarian) walked by a street vendor selling fried caterpillars. Wanting to do as the locals do, she tried one and thought it tasted like lobster. Meanwhile, half a world away in China, Rose was dared to eat a fried scorpion, and she thought it tasted like shrimp. When Laura and Rose got back to school, they started researching why people ate bugs in other parts of the world and not in America with a plan to form a company. They were joined by another student, Meryl Breidbart, and the trio experimented with insect-inspired foods. They tried everything from mealworm tacos to cricket sushi before landing on cricket powder, which they used to make America's favorite snack—chips! They entered pitch contests and eventually won enough money to fund their startup. But few people believed their insect-protein chips would be a success. Laura and Rose had to call four hundred tortilla-chip manufacturers before one was willing to make their chips. Laura and Rose appeared on *Shark Tank* and landed a deal with Mark Cuban. After a lot of hard work, their chips are now sold on thousands of store shelves across the nation, and their company has helped educate millions of people on how food impacts climate change.

You can learn more about their company at eatchirps.com.

HALLIE AND JAYE'S CRICKET COOKIE RECIPE

MAKES 24 LARGE COOKIES
TOTAL TIME: 1 HOUR

** Always ask an adult for help with preheating the oven and with placing the pans in and taking them out of the oven.

**Please do not use live or frozen crickets. Trust us, cricket powder works much better! You can find it online.

INGREDIENTS

- ½ cup salted butter
- ½ cup granulated sugar
- ¼ cup dark brown sugar
- ½ teaspoon salt
- 1 egg
- 2 teaspoons vanilla
- 1¼ cups all-purpose flour
- 1 teaspoon cinnamon
- ¼ cup *Chirps* cricket powder
- ½ teaspoon baking soda
- ⅔ cup chocolate chips

BAKING EQUIPMENT

- small and large mixing bowls
- measuring cup and spoons
- whisk
- wooden mixing spoon
- baking pan
- parchment paper
- oven mitts

DIRECTIONS

1. Microwave butter in a small bowl for 40 seconds, so butter is partially melted but not all liquid.

2. In a large mixing bowl, whisk together the granulated sugar, brown sugar, salt, and butter so there are no lumps.

3. Add in the egg and the vanilla. Then stir in the flour, cinnamon, cricket powder, and baking soda to form a dough (but don't overmix!). Add in the chocolate chips.

4. Chill dough in refrigerator for at least 30 minutes (longer is even better).

5. Preheat oven to 350°F (180°C).

6. Grease a baking pan or line with parchment paper so cookies don't stick to the pan.

7. Roll dough into small balls and place on pan with one inch between the cookies.

8. Bake in the oven for 8–10 minutes or until edges of cookies are golden brown. With oven mitts on, remove pan from oven.

9. Let cookies cool for 15 minutes (although we definitely sneak some hot!).

10. Eat! Bug appétit!

HEATHER TALKS WITH LAURA AND ROSE

Heather: I love your story! When I set out to write, I reimagined it as if you'd met in middle school instead of college. Did I get it right? Are Hallie and Jaye like you?

Laura: Yes! Growing up, I was the kid who wore a different shoe on each foot and came up with all these wacky ideas, just like Hallie does. My family was really quirky, too—we once had nine rats as pets! I was always comfortable being unique, but I also had to figure out how to fit in with kids who didn't see the world like I did, and sometimes that wasn't easy.

Rose: Jaye is *so* like me. As an immigrant kid, I have struggled a lot with my identity. I was born in China, and when we moved to America, I worked really hard to act like the American kids at school, but then when I went home, everything was very Chinese. I wanted to belong, so I tried to be what I thought others wanted me to be, which meant I acted differently for different people. It took me a long time to get comfortable with myself.

Heather: Tell me about the first time you two met. Were you instant friends?

Rose: I remember seeing Laura in our dorm hallway the first day of college. She was super sunny and really, really enthusiastic. And the first thing I thought was: "This girl must be fake."

Honestly, Laura was so different from anyone I'd ever met, and I didn't know what to make of her. On *Shark Tank*, Mr. Wonderful called Laura "Ms. Happy," and I think that's the best way to describe her. However, since I was insecure and only cared about fitting in, Laura's sunny disposition and very loud personality rubbed me the wrong way. It wasn't until a few months into college when I got some good news and Laura was happier for me than I was for myself did I finally realize how amazing Laura is as a person.

Heather: In the book, Hallie goes to the pitch competition wearing a cricket costume. Did you do that?

Laura: I did! Growing up, I was known for making costumes. If it was "wear red day" at school, the other kids would show up in a red shirt, and I'd show up in a full-out ketchup-bottle costume. I made a cricket costume and wore it to all our pitches. I even wore it on *Shark Tank*.

Heather: *Shark Tank* must've been amazing. Were you nervous to do your pitch in front of the Sharks?

Rose: I'm always nervous before a pitch, and I get this heavy swelling feeling in my chest. I've had to learn how to take that nervous butterfly energy and channel it into positive energy to use onstage.

Laura: I remember standing backstage and looking out at the Sharks, not believing I was really there. I knew how important it was to get the pitch right. We had one chance. There were no redos.

Rose: We'd practiced our pitch so much. Over and over. And we'd tested our chips on lots of kids, because they tell the truth. But that didn't stop me from having nightmares that one of the Sharks would take a taste and make a face and millions of people watching TV would see and that would be the end of our company.

Laura: But that didn't happen. They all really liked the chips. They understood what our product was about.

Heather: Were you entrepreneurs when you were kids?

Laura: I was without really knowing it. The kids on my block used to collect our old toys and throw garage sales. And I always had lemonade stands. When I was fifteen, I had a lemonade and cookie stand in the park. I got other neighborhood kids involved and we raised $14,000 to replace the old playground equipment there. When the Parks Department saw what I was doing, they chipped in money to install the equipment.

Heather: Wow! How did you make so much money?

Laura: Every morning, I baked dozens of cookies and made gallons of lemonade, then biked them to my stand in the park. I was there for nine hours every day for the entire summer. I was super committed—and I loved it.

Heather: What qualities do you think an entrepreneur needs to succeed?

Rose: An entrepreneur needs to be able to keep going, even when they get knocked down. It took us a lot of tries and a lot of experimenting before we found the right product.

Laura: Part of building a business is being willing to make mistakes and then learn from them and make changes. Remember my lemonade stand? The first time I did it, I charged only twenty-five cents a cup. That night, when I added up the money I made and compared it to the money I'd spent on the ingredients, I realized I'd lost money! So the next day, I raised my prices.

Rose: Wait! I thought of another important quality—being

able to work well in a team or group. It helped so much to have a partner. Laura and I each contribute a different set of skills. We've learned how to listen to each other.

Laura: And we have fun together.

Rose: We have so much fun together!

© Ben Von Wong

HEATHER ALEXANDER is the author of numerous fiction and nonfiction books for kids, including the Wallace and Grace series, The Amazing Stardust Friends series, and A Child's Introduction to . . . series. In addition to writing books, she also works as a children's book editor. She grew up in New Jersey and now lives in Los Angeles, California, with her family and beagle, Luna. Since meeting Rose and Laura, she can't stop munching on cricket chips while writing (cheddar is her favorite flavor).

Visit her at heatheralexanderbooks.com.